THE MEN IN MY LIFE

a novel

THE MEN IN MY LIFE

a novel

Deena Linett

for the women in my life

Contents

THE MEN IN MY LIFE

South Florida

When people hear my accent they imagine they know me, because they've seen a Tennessee Williams play or read Faulkner or Katherine Anne Porter, but her accent was a wild unlikely fusion of West Texas and Southern Belle bound to the expressive mind of a really interesting thinker.

There are countless Souths, and anyway I resist the gothic.

I'm so urban now that even my children barely credit my history, and friends here in New York can't imagine a girlhood so different from their own. A girlhood without overcoats, I think, every time it goes below freezing, place where I learned a great deal that isn't very useful here. I know about poisonous plants—oleander's particularly lovely—and deadly snakes: the coral snake, which doesn't even look dangerous, has a nerve agent that can kill you in seven minutes.

I know how to rock a car out of the sand.

The Gulf in which I swam naked at night—phosphor skimming my body with cool miraculous light—is unknown to the people I know now. Someday I would like to write about that, being washed in light.

You can't feel it, of course.

I grew up in a quiet unselfconscious Florida whose black population was invisible to me, a poor white child. Florida in the fifties doesn't know the Cubans are coming and hasn't the vision to imagine rich retirees, mostly Protestant, but significant numbers of Catholics and Jews as well. My Florida's flat and sandy, an unreflective place that in two decades will wake and flick its powerful tail like a hungry gator.

And ah, those years on the beach . . . ! Days we lay there telling dirty jokes – first place I heard of oral sex, though of course I couldn't imagine it properly. We'd comb peroxide through our hair—it made mine a bizarre pale carroty copper streaked with gold. There were dances on floors laid out on the sand, horns wailing, and soft wind on damp skin, press of boys' lumpy mystery against me, their hands on my back, and sweat a sweet second skin.

People laugh when I forget and slide into an occasional Southern idiom—I still sometimes say *y'all*. Stopped conversation dead in a café recently when with a whole crowd of friends talking about urban dangers and the proliferation of firearms, without thinking I let slip I know how to handle a rifle.

But the differentness is wonderful.

My practice—and of course my life—is rich with plural cultures. I'm easy with blacks and Cubans, people from the Islands. But with some Spanish-speakers from the Americas, not. In grad-school a black professor told me I have WASP distance-needs. I need more personal space than a lot of Latinos who sometimes stand too close. Or closer than I'm comfortable with. Sometimes this is cultural, sometimes it's class, sometimes simply personality— who knows.

And central to any sense of the Florida I come from is my first love.

Whew. I'd never written, or said, that before. Perhaps I hadn't truly known it.

Ciro Rodriguez-Playa: a brief history.

When I was seventeen and he was twenty-two we went out a few times. Apart from being thrilled by his interest, I have retained only the vaguest memories of those evenings. I do remember a powerful crush, a young man absolutely dizzying in his sexual appeal. And though it makes me wince now, a "catch."

Once we must've gone to a formal because I remember his dark face and jet hair above a white dinner jacket. And his body against mine. He was a *man*, older. Sexually experienced, which in the days of my euphemism-addled youth meant he was "mature." He had finished law school, and I was about to leave for college. When he kissed me again last year I remembered his kisses, the shape and taste of them. How could this have remained, the taste of him? Despite everything—a given evening's perfume and food, the passage of *decades*, illnesses and time, the repeated shocks of aging: there it was, his unique taste. I knew him.

This happens: we kiss and I'm a girl, he's a young man, unscarred, his life and all his time ahead.

I tasted something essential in him after thirty years.

Space-time curves. Even schoolchildren know this: mass reshapes the space around it. As if he were an object in the net of space-time, his presence flexed the walls and they became a little cup. I tumbled in.

We didn't sleep together in those days, when we were young. It wasn't done. All my girlfriends did it, but I was saving myself, saving "it"—absurd then, outright hilarious now—that marginal bit of tissue; astonishing and terrible the value some cultures still ascribe to it.

This was rural Florida at the end of the sixties, a hard place to be a Jew, which I am, and even harder to be a Cuban immigrant who's also a Jew, which Ciro is, technically, because his mother had a Jewish mother. But technically he's not even Cuban, because he managed by six hours to be born in the States. So he's marginally a Jew and marginally a Cuban. In light of these facts—life-facts determined utterly by chance— everything he does becomes predictable.

Actually everything's chance. If my parents had sneezed while they were making me, I might be a man, six feet tall.

Somewhere in the material about Ciro and me there is an explanation for why we never married but I didn't look for it then, and now it's not relevant.

Of course all this is just after Castro. I've wondered why his people didn't settle in Ybor City, but it's not the kind of thing one asks. The waves of immigration to Miami aren't going to happen till later, and when they do they will have an immense tidal pull on him, which for all these thirty-odd years will not have crossed my mind.

I never saw him again, Ciro, until my father died. Thirty-two years.

We had each married and divorced. In the years between he had the sons, and a daughter who died horribly in a game park in the Transvaal, an accident with a rhino. I imagine gored.

This is the sort of thing I heard when I visited home. And stories about his beautiful wife, affairs, difficulties. He ran for office. He won. He lost. His wife left him because of the succession of women. He married another beautiful wife. I heard but didn't attend; he was distant background and I was immersed in my own life and gathering my children.

After I saw him at the funeral I tried to recollect and sort what I'd heard over the years, but it was tatters: pictures in the social pages my parents had occasionally sent. Gossip from old friends and my people, then from my father and his new wife, after my mother died.

Ciro wears gold chains and a $75,000 Rolex watch that'd make me unbearably self-conscious. My stepmother was impressed by Ciro, impressed that I'd known him since high school. Maybe that's a reason we didn't consider marrying: everybody drags early class differences into adulthood, some integrating them more successfully than others. Differences in personal styles can get in the way, and here's something I know but fail to remember: if my name had been Gloria Esposito Ciro wouldn't have looked at me.

He needs to be flashy, unlike many—even most—immigrants, and I need to be fairly invisible. Which is pretty impossible with my masses of curly red hair, which I could cut short and do not. Which makes my much-cherished invisibility suspect.

A person can invent countless reasons for not doing something. More than thirty years later when I loved being in bed with him, I knew why I hadn't married him. Even young I had known him: he would have had to be unfaithful to a wife, and I could not have been that wife.

He stroked my face in the most wonderful and peculiar way when we made love. The flat of his palm pressed hard, he rubbed my cheek as if learning my bones—or shaping them. As if time were a patina he could erase, leaving me young and new and polished.

When he was doing it I almost didn't like it—it was too rough, even in the breathless ferocity of our desire: it was uncivil.

It told me how deeply I was wanted.

An instructive weekend. Sometime during it I understood he craved excitement. That was another reason: the most excitement I want is a visit from a hidden part of my mind. Or an unexpected phone-call. A trip. Though my life is mostly neatly ordered and predictable—close to but not quite at the point of boredom—I often surprise myself with something I say or do. This delights me. Irrespective of volition my mind occasionally does something inventive, possibilities of transformation well up, and I am satisfied. Once I heard a poet say *I love my interior.* Yes.

I love my subconscious. Sometimes I think it's all I have. Which is not the case, in fact.

Thirty-two years pass during which we do not think of each other. Or: I do not think of him. I am busy in the dailiness of my life, raising my children and divorcing and learning to be a therapist and focusing on my traffic. Typo! (God! What does *that* mean?) My *practice!* and doing some teaching at the Institute.

Lifetimes.

He is fifty-six and I am fifty-two. He is of course still swarthy, short—not the sort of man who usually appeals to me—a dark golden-brown color, like gingerbread. I am pale, slightly fatter than I'd like to be and getting paler. Redheads fade. In fact. And then continue to, so that sometimes when I look at myself in the mirror in the bathroom I think I will go invisible right before my eyes: one day I'll look and she—the me in the mirror—will disappear in the mist after the shower. Or I'll look and all I'll see is my mop of curls, my best feature. A free-floating red curly object—

springy ringlets—floating in the steam, no face under it, no body. Which is just as well, the shape it's in.

Ridiculous. I put my glasses on and there she is, middle-aged, fading, not slim enough. But I'm a shrink so I know: even when slim, I'm wasn't slim enough.

Which brings us almost to the present. I find myself in middle-age, youth having passed before I understood its velocity: it's so elastic, joyful, boundless that, because I wasn't thinking, I seem to have believed it would last forever.

It doesn't. I go to Sarasota for my father's funeral. My marriage and a love affair have gone, and I am not thinking of Ciro Rodriguez-Playa, who appears before me, stands too close, and is wearing—of all things—a trim little Hemingway beard and a softly crumpled fishing hat. Mercifully minus the hooks and flies.

I look at this man in the hat, but I am not expecting Ciro. I am grieving. I have flown down suddenly because at four that morning my stepmother had called and said, "Your daddy's had a heart attack," and I, moving into wakefulness, said "Will he live?"

"Why, honey, he's already day'ed."

The man stands too close. I back away, feeling a bit crowded, murmur "I'm sorry" preliminary to *I don't think I know you* when he says "How're you doing, darlin'?" and I cry "Ciro!" and, time collapsing, throw myself into his arms. His presence is absolute comfort. *Ciro.* I kiss him.

He comes to the house that night. My stepmother says did I know that when my father was coming out of anesthesia and still on the respirator he was panicky.

Why must she tell me this, my father *in extremis?*

She talks. Without ceasing. I can't excuse it by saying it's the way she grieves, and it's not something I can do anything about. I used to tell myself my father married her for the noise. She retells the horror story but here's a new piece: her voice softens, she looks at Ciro, and tells me, But Ciro came. I called him and he came. And he talked to your daddy and calmed him down. He was all right—she pauses for the pleasure of the drama—*after Ciro came.*

I look at him, but he doesn't meet my eyes, turns to get a drink. I very much want to see his dark and beautiful face.

I know he's drawn my father's will and over the years advised him. I do not yet know that he has loved my father. I am thinking about the moment at the door, minutes before, when I opened it and he walked in. He *picked me up*—astonishing—whispered "Hello, darlin," and rubbed his cheek against mine. "I bet you thought I'd forgotten."

Forgotten?

I simply had not thought of him in all these years.

Then he kissed me, and I recognized him.

Between Ciro and me there's a stream of clarity like summer rain.

Because it's always been so easy between us I've been surprised to have had to learn it with other men, with Terry, who I was married to for what I think of as the centerpiece of my life, certainly all my youth. Father of my children. We married when I was nineteen and separated pretty much by mutual consent after twenty-four years, though he was more in the grip of inertia than I was. We both knew the energy had gone out of the marriage, and I think what kept us together was our history with the children, and the familiarity. And kindness, though all the sparks had pretty much burned out. Or we used them up, I told him once, laughing and crying, On all those children.

I was forty-four then, and when I met Toss, as my marriage was ending, I knew I was crazy about him because no matter how close he stood, even when he breathed on me, I delighted in it. Toss, however, is another chapter.

It'd been eight years since I had lived with Terry when my father died and Ciro reappeared in my life. *The past is a foreign country.* In fact, though you bear its marks and its delicate traceries. With Ciro and me all the emotional parts fit.

And maybe none of the surface parts.

I remember feeling him tremble against me when we kissed on one of those nights when I was seventeen. I don't remember other men that way. I love him, I suppose.

I love that part of him that knows me.

He's a lawyer. We both went to college in Florida though he was in Gainesville and I went to Miami.

Then he went to grad school up North, to Columbia and NYU. A lot of Florida boys did that then; still do. His sons are at NYU doing a year in tax law. Then in my sophomore year I married Terry. I was a girl when I married, a child. If one of my daughters…they wouldn't dare. They wouldn't even consider it, they're way smarter than I was.

And at the same time, or intermittently, there's Liam, who's important.

And married.

I never forget that—how could I? And who would I be if I did?

Liam.

A silvery-gray current, as if wind made visible were material and male.

Over the years I've learned that if I write things out they get clearer. Which goes some way to explaining the writing: during the last six years or so I've published some short fiction and oddly, it's taught me about myself, even though none of the stories is about me.

With all those children they couldn't possibly be.

So okay: Liam. Of the beautiful body. And voice, deep and honey-colored, and lovely accent.

Do not edit.

I remember now: I'd been working on two short fictions when I began this piece about Liam—began it as a short story but it slid quite without my volition into first person—

This is not going to be the story of a wayward man—charming and brutal, a man with a magnetic aura driven by a kind of animal mindlessness. No. This is about an extraordinarily civilized man, a statesman. Who nevertheless like everyone else has a psychic underside: soft, deep red and veined. Marbled with fat. Meaty.

And here—I have to pause, having trouble taking a breath—here it is. I've unfolded the big manila envelope which I'd stashed against the side-wall in the cabinet behind me: the diary-entry I wrote about my— encounter? dalliance? — *event*— with Liam.

Which I'd forgotten till I needed to remember it.

I'm a psychologist: forgetting is data for something.

Rereading, I'm stricken. What an image: Raw and fleshy and animal. All the things sex is about, for me.

And for him.

If truth be told my entire life has been determined by sex. I sometimes think.

Of course at other times I reckon it differently. How is it possible that a most intangible and mysterious aspect of personality so determines us?

I'm an accomplished professional woman, so some of the time I think this is funny, and at other times I can barely keep from wailing: what does it mean, sex? surrounds and scents, sounds, the very specific touchings and tastes?

I know what it means.

It's the life-force working through us, using us, and for someone who believes, against a whole lot of evidence, in free choice, this *requiring* is absolutely unacceptable.

And human nature, so at this late stage, you ought to accept it, E.

In Liam's Country

I telephoned to say I was in his country, and if he had a chance…

He was glad to hear from me, he said. He'd see what could be arranged.

Immediately I felt calling him had been a mistake.

Two hours later his secretary phoned to say he'd meet me at the National Museum.

When I saw him I would not ask for his wife, and he would not say, though in the e-mail telling him I would be coming, I'd written, *if you and Mary are in X…*a city not far from the capital.

I'd met Mary, a tiny woman like a doll whose big beautiful daughter, serving tea, had seemed a young goddess.

Goddesses, unlike women, remain young eternally—or the daughter is the eternal part of the mother. (In fact: mitochondria). I was captivated by the girl's reality: nineteen, the daughter was huge and full-breasted, her long neck brushed by coiled reddish-brown curls, a fleshly impossible issue from Mary's elegant narrow loins.

I wasn't, at the time, thinking of my daughters.

She was breathtaking.

Once upon a time I was that beautiful, I thought—a flash—and immediately knew I couldn't credit it.

Dressing, redoing my makeup, I remembered something Georgia O'Keeffe had said: *After New York I always think European cities are like villages.* So I decided to be resolute—but about what? —and unimpressed by the secretary, though the hills on the horizon, and the colors in the sky, were marvelous.

He was one of the five senior people in his country's present government. I read about him at home all the time.

There'd been a recent article about his being on the board of the very museum where I was going to meet him. A purchase of three Sisley oils for $6.2 million led highly placed people to object: the money could have been better spent. His response was a curt statement to the effect that every culture on Earth produces art, so "we must infer that it is needed," and then something about how this country in particular needed art as counterweight. To terrorism, he meant, but one wouldn't say that.

I thought about the Towers. I frequently think about the Towers—I'm a New Yorker now, they'd belonged to me too.

There was a taxi rank across from the hotel, and because I didn't know how close the museum was, I was early. But nothing is wasted. I saw the incredible skeleton of an Irish elk, or red deer, the label said, fully seven feet tall—*when dressed,* I thought, amused. The note said it'd gone extinct in the late Quaternary Ice Age. And we? I thought. When will we go extinct — which did away right quickly with the laughter. And then here he was, rushing toward me, big and energetic, hearty. He kissed me fast and, arm around my shoulders, directed me along the passageway out, down the steps and into the street. "We'll get a coffee."

Men don't ask, I thought, unreasonably short of breath, telling myself *It's his pace,* and having to skip a little to keep up. A man of average height, thick-set and sturdy, he moved with long strides, leaning forward as if in a great hurry. Or at something crucial. I remember thinking that.

At the coffee-bar he talked about politics in this, his country, of the situation for the government (shaky, but shaky'd become the norm), of his work at the university where, visiting to give a talk last year, I'd met him.

I ordered Darjeeling tea and we split a sandwich drenched in mayonnaise, picking at a tangle of thick oily chips.

Afterward I wondered whatever had possessed me. I sprinkled a ring of sugar around his cup. If he asks, I thought, I'll say I was thinking of ancient stone circles.

It was to keep him safe.

I remember thinking this.

To keep him?

He watched, didn't ask. Perhaps I made it for myself as well. They say that here: *as well. Oh, aye.*

"Have you been dancing at all?"

I looked at him, surprised, and feeling—all the while this was going on—over-large and graceless, because of Mary.

The wife. Mother of his children. The woman with whom for more than thirty years. Beautiful and fey Mary. And I? I am thick, ordinary as clay. Lush, I might say in a different context, abundant. But here in Mary's slender shadow—in her place—I was, though small, over-large.

"I am going to take you dancing."

We'd danced last time, wild and slightly drunk, to jazz and familiar rock. *I'm from where it was invented!* We'd whirled and spun and swung, and I couldn't take my eyes off him, the most sexually overt dancer in my experience—but only I knew it: nothing in his movements looped beyond the two of us, and because we'd all been drinking I was sure it had nothing to do with me. It's that male performance-thing, I told myself, short of breath, sweating. I remember sweating.

So then we were out on the street, and I heard myself say "You are the most opaque man I have ever in my life met," thinking, In a long line of opaque men.

"Am I, then? Good."

Truth was, I'd phoned him because of the dancing, as if something had not happened that was meant to.

During both visits I'd heard people in this country talk about "The Americans" as if it were possible to characterize us. Occupied by images of the Great Plains, the hills around San Francisco, the long humid stretch along the river at Memphis, stands of bamboo and reaches of orange groves in South Florida where I grew up, the High Line in New York, where I live now, occasionally I tried to imagine myself as Europeans saw me. If I knew that, it'd redefine the way I see myself, and anyway, I did it too: "the Brits, the French, the Swedes." I once heard a Dane say, "The Swedes are the Germans of Northern Europe."

We walked. It was nearly nine and getting dark. He hailed a taxi and then just as abruptly ordered it to stop where the buildings were crowded together and traffic in the streets denser. City Centre, a sign said. I stood with him in the street, a bit dazed, as if I'd drunk more than tea. The sky had gone from rosy lakes with gold edges to smoke-gray streaked purple.

"We'll go for a drink." He nodded in the direction of a dark ramshackle place that could've passed for a construction fence. "It's famous."

This? Place that at home would be very downtown, I thought, trying to find something unique in the dark façade.

"The Crown," he said with a compact gesture, "Been in several films, it's in the Historic Trust," and pushed the battered wooden door open into a wide shadowy space.

As my eyes adjusted I was able to make out what looked like a collection of little rooms to the right and left against the walls. The bottom parts of these were dark wood, but the tops seemed to be half-walls of glass that glittered with curlicues and festoons in dark reds and golds and emeralds that would prevent anyone seeing inside. "These are for assignations," he said, steering me into one. There were benches and a broad table. I sat. The ornamented half-walls obscured us entirely. "Now no one will know you're here," he said.

I laughed and laughed, nearly said it: I'm not the one who has to hide.

He went to get drinks and came back with them to sit, his thigh against mine, in the little room.

I talked about my children, aware of his thigh. About my work, and it was easy, as if we hadn't lived entire lives separated by an ocean.

When he talked about duplicity among particular colleagues he leaned his head against mine and lowered his voice, so that the rumble of his words vibrating in my bones became my own thinking. The Government needed to depend upon certain people, and could not. "We find ourselves in a bit of a muddle," he said, drawing diagrams of relationships in the wet on the dark tabletop. Without thinking I understood outlines of what he hadn't said. His party had constructed a coalition among several of the five major parties, had distributed what at home were called perks, offices and secretariats, governorships, and ministries; now he was—or someone was—about to call in the chips. I sensed rather than thought this.

The government is his life, I understood, watching him in the murky light, wondering what kind of man runs governments—visionary or statesman? Poor at intimacy? Poor at being a husband?

No matter.

Or, it isn't relevant, I remember thinking.

He rose, finishing his drink. "I'll get us another," and before I could say no, he strode out to the bar, and returned with someone. "This is Francis," he said, and though his eyes were steady, and his face, I knew that wasn't the man's name.

I've been brought along to a political assignation, I thought, surprised and immediately chilled: Francis's eyes were pale and without expression. He nodded as they slid into the seats, Francis holding a Guinness which he lifted in greeting. "*Fáilte.*" He nodded, but my face felt frozen. Welcome. I felt my head dip without volition.

I think I registered something—a vacancy?— before I realized what it was. This man, this "Francis," brought into the present someone I'd met years before, in college, a man named Ulf, my first meeting with someone without beliefs. Without a spiritual life. Without—something essential. I'd never be able to identify it, but I'd recognized it even as a girl. And here it was again, in this dark little half-room built for political subterfuge, and the sexual.

Francis said a few things to Liam in a low voice, his accent heavy—or perhaps he wasn't speaking English—I couldn't've said what happened between them, but then he rose, extended a hand—I had to take it—and left.

Of course, I thought, when Liam said "Let's go. Across the street they have dancing." Of course he wouldn't explain.

I followed him into the chill urban dark.

"The most bombed hotel in Europe," he declared with a sweeping gesture. Headlines: **American Among Casualties in Hotel Bombing. Found with Statesman. Both Dead.**

I certainly hoped. The children would be mortified.

I followed him through a lobby gleaming with polished brass and a multiplicity of little lights—they call them fairy lights here—into the bar, where the space between us was oddly cool, as if we were still outdoors. I ordered a cordial. He looked quizzical, but I didn't understand until it came, and I tasted it.

"How is it?"
"Oh, it's fine," I told him.

"It's not fine," he said, bringing the glass to his lips. "It's..."

"...like children's cough syrup!"

"I shall get you something else."

"At home, cordials are liqueurs..."

I said yes to sherry and sipped it, embarrassed and giddy. I didn't say it tasted like ground gemstones. He didn't speak for some minutes and I didn't feel the need to.

We drank, memories of our laughter and the rhythms of our having danced together moving through, and when he rose and held out his hand, I could feel myself moving into his energy, wondering if I'd be able to keep up.

"This is what I wanted," I told him, aware of his breadth in my breast and belly. He pulled me closer, a man with a great deal of body-heat. I let myself move against him as if we'd been intimate for years.

"I want to take you upstairs."

"What's the point?"

"American," he said softly, chuckling.

I couldn't quit. "You're married. It won't mean anything."

"Of course it means something."

"I say too much."

"You do." He pulled me closer.

"It'll be a fling." I meant, for you.

He kissed me into silence, there on the dance floor. Briefly but wetly.
"Don't cause an international incident," I told him, withdrawing a bit.

"Well then, I suggest you comply," he smiled, utterly charming, radiant, male, confident. "Come."

"How could I not?" I said, more to myself than him, pressing against his side as we walked.

In the hotel room we met and tumbled in a whirl of animal warmth and necessity, and afterward I thought I should have heard a door slamming, the door that shut out thinking. In bed with him I was mindless, young, beautiful—or would have been, had I thought.

The next morning he said "I shall take you to see palm trees."

What?! *Majorca?* I thought. *Portugal?* We drove up to the north coast of his country, the sky low and boiling silver, and there they were, in the sea-spray, shabby, beaten by wind. Palms. In Northern Europe.

The next days back in my hotel I made a few jottings, which later became the pages I had in my hands. I remember thinking I'd been left with one loud question: how does your wife know who to be afraid of? Surely some women you meet for dinner—or luncheon or tea or drinks—are safe. Probably those are the ones you tell her about.

Reading it now, I think the story had a great deal to do with Ciro. But that's retrospective, because I met Liam—I was in his country—before I went home to my father's funeral and was confronted (!) by Ciro. And I know now that I couldn't have chosen Ciro all those years ago because if I had, I wouldn't've been able to bear it.

Liam is a beautiful and very appealing man. I took him for himself. I have been aware for some years that I welcome new experience. Life is short, and one should seize every safe possibility (this is not something I'd ever tell a client, but it's apt for me). But of course once you're involved with someone it's no longer safe: emotional involvement—even without the sexual—is risk.

And—this is ugly and hard to say—though contemplative by nature, a person whose brightest moments are often in the mind, I am drawn to men engaged by the exercise of power.

Drawn to them despite the many and obvious negatives. I don't like their turbulent style, the way they use people.

Sometimes they don't even *see* them.

I don't like their showiness and their cavalier offhand use of colleagues, serving people, even people closest. This awful thing happens: they begin to treat intimates as if they were sources, assistants. They use stratagems. It's a rare man committed to power and influence who doesn't do this.

As for my alliance—shall I call it?—with Liam, I felt that those days, days of my sexuality, were nearly over. I had already noted the beginnings of dryness and sometimes I nearly drowned in grief—all that slackening and shrinkage—right there on the horizon and growing closer. Godawful. Everything of deepest meaning would diminish, go, evaporate. Vanish. I wish I didn't know this: fat tissue actually replaces the milk-glands, those little interior rivers and their marvelous tributaries.

There's always, I begin to see, been Ciro.

How can a vast interior landscape have been so unavailable, so buried?

I get up and walk around.

I put on music.

I need silence.

A lot of time passes.

I look out the windows onto my city. New York is not a beautiful place—or mostly it's not, apart from the fabulous Cloisters and Central Park and the High Line and an occasional little park that you come upon, surprised. Mostly my famous city is like an illustration for heavy metal music: Ninth Avenue. Ugly storefronts with loud neon. But such riches! Everything you could ever want, from specially-colored two-cent buttons from Bangladesh to a five-carat cabochon diamond. The great glass-and-granite façades monuments to greed. And capital. And in Chelsea or SoHo, until recently you could break your ankle on the crumbling cobbles, and with all this, it's still—unlike the small town where I grew up—a place of infinite possibility.

Choices of all kinds and relentless energy. Novelty. A person needs that. And I see now, looking into the familiar cityscape, there's always been Ciro.

Whom I had not thought of—and never wanted—during all the years of my adult life.

Gaynell's the only one I can talk to about all this, but I'm not ready to. To try to put it into words will diminish—or fail to convey—the magnitude of what-all I'm realizing. Gaynell grew up in what she calls a micro-town on Blanche Bay, says she gets off a plane into sodden country air, the trees garlanded with Spanish moss, and she's home. "You get imprinted by your home-place," she said once. "Doesn't even have to be beautiful. It just has to be the right smells, or where the trees—oh, here we go—where the *land* has familiar features, a certain configuration. It's an animal thing. You want to go back because it's home."

"Like salmon." I remember I laughed.

"Swimming upstream," she muttered.

"And anyway," she added in her apparently languid Louisiana drawl, "How else could you possibly explain Neb-*ra*-ska?"

Behind that drawl is a mind like a box-cutter. I told her that once and her eyes went *wide.*

Then she said, "Magnetic fields. As for migration."

I remember saying "Every time I hear 'migration' I think *My gracious.*"

"That's why you write," Gaynell said. "Yes indeedy. *My gracious* indeed."

At different times in my life "home" has meant different places. Shouldn't it be fixed? One hearth, one place, perhaps, of origin?

"You know what?" I interrupted her because it seemed a startling thing: "He didn't teach it to us, my father thought we couldn't learn a thing." He didn't understand how we take in the world.

"That's where you come by your sense of responsibility," Gaynell said.

"Thank you, *Doctor.*"

Gaynell didn't have a daddy. She was raised by her grandpeople, her daddy's parents, after her momma died when she was eleven. "My old people had to put up with alla my teenage kiniptions." Or, thoughtful, she'd add, "My poor old people," sometimes in jest, sometimes with absolute empathic seriousness.

We met in training and we've been through a lot together. I do love her, Gaynell Porter-Adams. Main differences between us are, she's managed to stay married to her first original husband, and Gaynell and Coleman Adams chose not to have children.

Which means their marriage can retain its central place in their lives. When you have children everything gets diffuse while you're raising them. More accurate: knocked apart. Think "break" as at a pool-table.

Those years astonish me: even though I was fully present, I cannot fathom how I lived through them.

I wonder about Gaynell's and Coleman's lives sometimes, so focused on each other, so quiet.

In the months after my father's funeral and before I see him again, Ciro and I talk several times. He calls. He has managed to tell me he's no longer married, but I don't take in its significance. I hear him bringing me up to date, an old family friend. In contrast to his showiness with the jewelry and cars and clothes, his language is flat, oblique. You could miss a lot.

I did.

We have my father's estate to talk about—he's drawn all the documents, wills and trusts and estate plans—and he talks a bit about himself, the two heart surgeries, a bit about the failure of his second marriage. I think there's a subtle strain of responsibility for the loss of that wife. Nothing about political or other troubles. He has invited me to meet him when he's in New York to see his sons, but I'm going to be away and we'll miss each other.

This does not seem important. None of it does. Later I will ask myself why I hadn't thought of him sexually during all those little encounters.

Once he says something unmistakable. When I thank him for what-all he's doing for me he replies *You could thank me with sexual favors.* He delivers his sentence in his wonderful southern accent which is so familiar I almost never hear it. I hear the smooth southern gentleman, the hard-drinking playboy, the politico. It does not occur to me that he could be serious.

In training and analysis I learned a lot about denial. I'm very good at it. I assemble brilliant intellectual superstructures, ornate and fully elaborated, in place of the thing I'm busy denying. Their shapes and surface textures are so interesting I forget to look inside.

Sometimes I think they're like a concert grand: massive and polished, capable of evoking a world of sound. And what am *I* doing? I'm admiring the ivory keys and thinking about endangered African elephants—or hearing childhood in my head, someone playing "Chopsticks."

So now I'm in Sarasota again. I've told him I'm coming and he says he'll take me to dinner. Then he drives to the beach. He isn't crazy about the beach but he knows I am. He shows me a motel he owns, and that one, pointing, in which he has shares with a group of people who invest in real property along here. It isn't interesting, but because I'm with him attending to his voice and his rhythms and his accent, I listen hard. I hear everything he says, and a lot he doesn't.

We walk onto the sand. The waves gleam white where they froth and fall. The water's lit here and there with phosphor and gleams like starshine, little streaks and shimmers. When I was a teenager—before the hotels that line the sand—I used to go skin-swimming here with my friends. What a rowdy group of girls we were! Sometimes we'd go with boys, a big risk in those days. Once Maryellen lost her glasses in the sand. Once Jane—poor beautiful Jane, dead of cancer at forty-eight—lost her car keys. Sprays of recollection, swift and transitory as light on the water: we made a human chain, eight or ten or twelve girls, beautiful and young, our flesh positively radiant, and gloriously unselfconsciously firm, looking for the keys or the glasses. We found one but not the other, and I don't remember which.

We were so gorgeous in that taut young skin, and absolutely stupid: we didn't know how beautiful we were. We worried about pimples and when our breasts would stop growing, and whether a boy could tell if you'd fallen off the roof, local slang for having your period.

Once I brought my husband here at night to walk into the warm Gulf, but Terry was from Toledo, and he wasn't easy with the water, which he kept calling the ocean or the lake. Each time it was absolutely necessary to correct him: *the Gulf.* He worried about rays and sharks and wanted me to come out. At some point—I don't remember when this started—I began to go into the water. I have to walk into it when I come home, my Gulf, blue and easy.

Ciro and I walk along the cool packed sand at the wrack-line and I'm thinking it's utterly gorgeous and beautiful and romantic—I'm thinking what would it be like to make love with him right here on the damp sand?

It never occurs to me that he might be thinking it too. We're walking on the beach, Ciro and I, but we are old now, in our fifties. We do not hold hands. It is so beautiful and such a miracle to be with him that for a while I don't grieve my age.

Maybe he has a woman; certainly he has had many women, glamorous and beautiful and slim women. Young women. He's a public servant, an elected official. He has a driver and a state car. But tonight he's driving his baby-blue Cadillac, embarrassing, like the Rolex, this need for presentation amplified by—what? inherited Latin taste?—outrageous and unacceptable.

The baby-blue car's like a tank and dwarfs an already small man. I'm carrying my shoes in my hand and I walk in and out of the little waves lapping the sand.

"I love it here," I tell him, unnecessarily.

"I know you do."

At the beach I'm something other, unaware of my earth-bound self. Pure essence. I'm without age or time or experience at the edge of the Gulf. It's the only place—except in sex, and sometimes when working or writing and it's going well—where I'm fully myself. And when the children were small. Then too I was completely *in it,* caring for them. Seems a really long time ago—

He says he's bought a big house fourteen miles east. "Why live here if you're not on the beach?" I ask. He laughs.

I am not thinking about adult sex with him, but girl-things. I want to kiss him. I want to hold him, feel him against me. I want him near. Now that he's back in my life I will need to keep him in it.

We walk. I understand that in some way I have always missed him. His accent is the sounds of home. My father's dead now, and my mother has been gone for nearly twenty years. Rachel's dead and my sisters have moved to Arizona (*but it has no ocean!* I yelped) and Mississippi. He's all that's left. Even a raggedy past is yours.

In fact home is hugely changed. It's a city now, a tourist-destination. Earlier I drove out to Midnight Pass, where we used to swim in high school. Once upon a time it was empty and flat, a few clumps of sea-grape and patches of crabgrass growing in the sand, and I couldn't help myself: alone in the car I groaned. The new road has three lanes for traffic, and white-painted arrows telling you to turn left to go over the bridge at Stickney Point or straight to where the island goes under the waves and becomes a sand-bar before it rises again at Casey Key, a few miles south. All the places of my youth have been built on, planted, and paved over.

It's not that I want it all back—it's just gotten incomprehensible. Like the world. The recognition of which is a function of age. It's as if the palms were a fan that opened to let the wind through, and in the brief time before they close again, I can see Florida in the fifties and sixties, Cinderella before the ball. Before the transformation, to be more accurate. Which precedes the ball. And which is given her by a fairy godmother.

I try to tell him this, en Español. He chuckles. I speak a kind of corrupt, poor-folks' Spanish, ungrammatical and slangy, with—he says—a taste of black beans, "Tu Español suena como frijoles negros," and laughs.

"I don't belong anymore," I tell him, "Even this place—home—with its beautiful familiar trees, doesn't belong to me."

Ciro says "Nor me."

Does anything belong to you? I think, before I realize: He's been working his whole life to make it belong to him. I feel as if I'm choking.

Though intuitive and canny, he is, I think, absolutely unsophisticated in the devious inventive mechanics of mind.

As he says "I want you to have something" I am struck by a powerful recognition: he knows absolutely *nothing* about me. He knows how many children I have, but not their names or how I got them.

He does not know any lady-shrinks, I think, probably doesn't know any male ones either. It turns out I'm wrong about this, but his friends aren't academics and writers, the people I spend my life with. I make a mental note to send him my book, a collection of short stories that won a small national prize, but I never do, though I can't say why. He lives in popular culture, reads biographies of political figures and big fat books on American history. He goes to a lot of movies. His wives, when he had them, served on committees and wore the latest clothes, whereas I no longer know—or care?—I guess I care *some*—what's *in*.

I serve on committees too, professional ones, in contrast to the committees of the succession of his wives who donated time to poor people and to raising money for civic events like city-wide Christmas decorations, and spent their Thursday mornings at garden clubs. I know all this because as our fortunes rose a bit my mother aspired to these things, and finally belonged to some of them, the civic committees. Poor momma.

I tried, too. I really did try. Could not. Because it wasn't interesting, I told myself, but now I think it's just possible that I failed so I could leave it all behind and find a social context that suited.

"What?"

"I have something for you."

It's too dark to see his eyes. He's between wives. I don't know what this could possibly mean.

"It's too dark to see, Ciro," I murmur, at the edge of irritation.

"You're walking on it." I stop, look down at my bare feet in the sand gleaming in the pale light of a pink-and-dark night sky. "What? Have you dropped something?"

I feel a rush of angry confusion as he laughs. He laughs and laughs. He throws back his head, laughing.

"Ciro!"

"You're walking on it," he says again.

Frustrated and annoyed I plop down onto the cool sand.

"Now I'm sitting on it, right?" What could he possibly be talking about? I am imagining a blue velvet box with—a talisman. In that moment it comes to me that I would like to have a gold ring for my little finger. A thick gold ring, not like a marriage-band, but something heavy and memorable, like a signet ring. Bizarre. Maybe he's thinking a necklace, something like that.

"In fact…"

I wait. I hate puzzles and games. He loves them.

"I have bought you this strip of sand so you'll have your own beach," he says, soft.

I can't breathe.

I look up. He's standing above me, his pants-legs rolled up, his white shirtsleeves also.

My eyes are pouring tears. Without volition they are flooding my face and I am on my feet hugging him and crying and saying "Oh Ciro, you gave it back to me," and later I will realize he gave me what he himself could never have. Child of immigrants, he would work and earn, laboring like the poorest cane-cutter, and earn and buy and show, and he would own a lot of land, but he would never believe it was really his.

He nearly was a cutter of cane. His father grew sugar down near Clewiston. Later he had groves—stately march of fruiting trees for miles—up north in Lake County. There were groves in Winter Haven and a stretch near Orlando: he must've made a ton of money when Orlando boomed. Ciro, that is. His father was gone by then, dead in some byzantine Cuban rescue plot the details of which my father once tried to explain to me.

He held me hard and I wanted him with pure youthful fury.

We drove back. I couldn't quiet my rushing and thudding. *The beach.*

Into the roaring silence of the car moonlight poured its green-white light on my hands in my lap, the hands without the blue velvet box, hands full of sand. "Oh," Ciro said as we got to the causeway bridge to the mainland, "There's this." He wriggled to reach into a pocket and tossed a small manila envelope onto my lap—heavy for its size. "This is the rest of it."

"Rest?"

"Open, my lady."

We'd driven onto the bridge. I held the thing in my hand and looked out at the water, black with the moon's lovely glittery pathway on it, a fringe of low city lights like the rhinestones I wore in high school strung along edges of the dark.

In the daytime the water's bluegreen and turquoise and navy blue, with yellow in the shallows and over sandbars. I could feel a small flat thing through the paper.

He glanced at me as we swung around onto Palm Avenue.

"I can't." I was crying hot tears.

Grief, it felt like.

He reached his arm out and pulled me toward him on the massive front seat. It was a different touch from the hugs, the kisses. More requiring. I knew we would go to bed then. It was—awful word—more like ownership.

I leaned against him, unable to stop crying.

"Open it," he said again.

A key.

"Key goes to the place."

"Place," I repeated like a stupid child.

"The one that goes on top of the sand," he grinned.

In the future I would think how much pleasure he'd taken to put this gift together—for me. At the time I was a mess, crying and laughing and streaming tears. It was all tangled together, as later our breath, our arms and legs.

"It's a condo—small. You won't be able to have all your kids there at once," he said. "It's in Spindrift," one of the buildings he owns.

"Oh my dear God!" I managed, fumbling for tissues. Meanwhile we were driving south of town, past the turnoff to my stepmother's place, where I was, theoretically, staying.

"I'll have to call her," I said.

"I suppose." It wasn't his problem.

I couldn't see enough to know if my makeup was all smudged; surely it was. "I don't have a change of clothes, or a toothbrush…"

He looked at me directly and laughed, and then he pulled in to a drugstore, where I ran in and got a few things. Including condoms. I just knew it: he was really put out when I showed him later, but I was thinking, Tough if you don't like it, Ciro-baby, but I gotta take care of myself, hardly able to keep from laughing.

"Place down near Venice," he said, when I got back into the outlandish car.

I nodded. Finally, quieting—everything was serious now—I asked, "How can I ever possibly thank you for this?"

He looked at me again, lights from the other cars along the South Trail periodically splashing brightness across his dark familiar face. "It's my pleasure, darlin.'"

New York and Elsewhere

I woke with the pressure of his thigh between mine, the wonderful texture of his skin. It was remarkable, the textures and tastes and the way we were together, a mix of ferocity and breathtaking tenderness.

The light came in gray through curtains. Here he was, a boy I'd been crazy about but hadn't slept with then, and now time, terrible and generous, had given him to me again. A well-loved man was holding me, in the present of my life. It wasn't the Red Sea parting, but it felt like a miracle.

I laughed.

"¿Qué?"

"It's a miracle," I said into his neck.

"Poquitico."

"Not a real one?"

"Real enough," he said, rolling to lie on top of me and look into my face. He rubbed my cheek with his. Stroking his back I felt the scars, imagined him drained and white, in that terrible sleep.

I opened my legs.

The crush and need when I was young had returned, but differently. It was beautiful and unpredictable. And dangerous; I knew that now. Like mercury? I wonder what I ought to know about mercury. Desire like a rare metal. Like a mirror in which the past shimmers but the future's smudgy.

I was wiping my glasses on my skirt when it came to me again. I asked, "Do you realize that had we been born in an earlier time…"

"We'd be dead," he offered cheerily.

"Without glasses, I'd've been a depressive. Imagine all that darkness, those little windows…I think about that a lot…"

"Are you depressed?"

"No, but I mean, without the development of technologies—"

"I would've died a long time ago." As he spoke his voice drifted off. I watched his eyes as he went somewhere and returned.

"You would've been illiterate," he said.

"You wouldn't have," I said, thinking of his drive, naming it for the first time.

"No?" he laughed. "I'd've been somebody's campesino…"

"Do you know what? I always think of your mother as a Cuban noblewoman."

"Do you." I guess he'd learned it in politics: never let anybody see your surprise.

"I think of her as large—as if she were a very tall woman, with grand regal bearing."

"Mamacita?"

"Does he want to marry you?" Gaynell asked, when I told her about the beach.

"Of course not. He doesn't know the first thing about me. He doesn't even know my children's *names*."

"But a house too?"

"It's a small condo…you can use it, Gay! You and Coleman can take vacations down there—it'll be great!"

"But why?" She hesitated—she's much more confrontive and willing to say than I am—and finally asked "What've you done to earn it?"
"Gay*nell!* That is a *terrible* question!" I dissolved into fits. "I'm a good lay, I reckon."

"You are shameless."

"It's a good question."

"You haven't asked yourself?"

"It seemed perfectly natural." Ordained. Or-dained?

"Probably you should."

"Mm-hm."

"People don't just up and hand you over a valuable property and a condominium without expecting something." She shook her head, jet hair swinging.

"I've been telling you, Gaynell, he's ostentatious." And loving and generous, I was beginning to see. It would be necessary to think about "ordained," a word that came from nowhere I'd ever been.

New York, November, rainy, cold, and blowy. I was working hard, in my practice and on some new stories. After years without anybody in my life now I had two amazingly beautiful and important men linked by having occurred close together, like earthquakes and tidal waves.

I'll say.

Loving them had shifted all the relationships in my life. Whenever I thought of either of them, I imagined physical upheaval, and grinned. And never failed to be aware that one of the beautiful men was not free and the other was someone I'd known all my life, and maybe not free either; I sensed a woman at the periphery.

I never kidded myself. I had no business messing with Liam, but sometimes I'd think of our ride to see palm trees, and an afternoon in a town called Limavady.

"This place is so lovely—" I stopped, realizing it was quite unnaturally still. Like a stage-set before the actors come on, and the grass a most vibrant green.

"Like Brigadoon," said Liam. "Places that disappear when we don't walk their streets."

"When we don't live in them," I added, aware then of a large political truth. "We're getting into social theory here," I said.

"Oh aye. And political theory."

Our talk was like that, spatterings of large things, most of the content of which was unsaid—very odd. I remember grinning up at him: "I like it," and he nodded, taking me by the shoulders and striding forward.

It had all in fact happened—to me. We ate there and held hands on the street. Whitewashed little houses hard against the street rising from land that looks flat but isn't: it's hilly in the way that the land must be where the Vietnam Memorial rises out of what you haven't realized is a concavity. And occasionally sex with him would move through me with a kind of terrible power, and I'd feel it between my legs or in my breast or arms, and long for him, a brief gust, nothing I held onto or tried to build on. If I could... what? A fragile summer house? A bright glass house, miraculous and temporary

I was doing my work, dealing with an especially difficult supervisee I thought probably shouldn't be a therapist, and worried about what to do about him. I'd have to talk to Gaynell, and found myself wishing for my dear colleague, William, who had died. Whose voice I will never hear again, whose pleasure in hearing my voice on the phone remains, though I can no longer conjure the sounds of it. "*El-eh*-na!" he'd say, ringing with gladness. "*El-eh*-na, how *are* you?" and he really wanted to know.

William's another form of Liam, like Guillaume. Stephen is Etienne. Saul of Tarsus changed his name to Paul, to Christianize it. I know all sorts of absolutely irrelevant stuff. I know about an Asian language, though I can't remember which, that has no straight lines, so it could be written on banana leaves without tearing them. I loved William, who was completely without that awful posturing. Or, being much older, he'd completely outgrown it. Or, who knows who William was when he was young.

In grad school when I first began writing, I'd bring my short stories to him. It wasn't till I was doing the post-doc, working with Charles, that I wrote about myself. I wonder if things would have been easier had those two kinds of writing been reversed. But they weren't, and I didn't know Charles yet.

Once over lunch in a grungy diner up in Morningside Heights William told me an awful story from his practice. For the first time in all the years I'd known him, he warned me—remarkable word. Must've been remembering William's warning when the telephone rang, or time pleats and brings two edges together, and I thought I'd been thinking about him when the phone rang, but probably I remembered it all afterwards—"You will not tell anybody this," he said. "I will never open a collection of your fiction and find this story in it."

"You won't." I nodded. "Then what happened?" I asked, about the unspeakable events he'd just recounted.

He shrugged, palms up and open, "You know men."

"No, William, in fact I do not know men."

So how can I be a therapist? How dare I write?

Dear William. Sometimes I've looked for him in the sky.

In fact.

For him and for Toss.

What I'm trying to get back to—and resisting: the telephone rang at 9:10 a.m. in my office.

"We know you know Liam," said a voice.

I froze. Then water—hot and freezing, both—felt like it poured down my neck and arms.

"We know you know Liam, and we want you to ask him to meet someone at…"

I reached for a pen, but my hand was having a violent spasm, so I knocked over the black cup with a dozen pens in it.

"Wait—! I'm trying to write down what you're saying…"

"The Coca-Cola bottling plant to the west of the town. He knows it." That was all.

Oh God, I thought, sitting. *The Coca-Cola plant*—if it weren't horrifying it would've been funny, a rhetoric thirty years old.

It's a mistake, I told myself.

This is my *life*, I remember thinking in a surge of pure mad panic, not a spy novel. Breathe. Breathe, E.

I'll call, I thought, and he won't be there.

You do not know that, I told myself.

Another wave of chills moved through me, down my arms: I remembered the man with the stone eyes, *Francis*, and felt my shoulders draw up.

You are here, I told myself, deliberate. What sort of message could I possibly leave with a secretary? I'd sound like a desperate lover.

My accent works against me here, as in other serious moments.

I thought—irrelevantly—about "entangling alliances" and briefly wondered which American document it's in. Or—then I began to laugh and laugh, my eyes running tears—it'd be as if I were a girl, calling to say I've missed a period.

I'd call his house and when his wife answered I'd just matter-of-factly say I'm Elena Summerfield, and I met your husband at a conference sponsored by his university last year, and someone has just telephoned with a message.

Can't do it.

The pens and pencils lay like pick-up-sticks. If I moved the wrong one there'd be an explosion.

Over time the chills and shaking slowed, though I remained at the desk staring at the telephone like an idiot. My still telephone like a bomb.

Which might go off if I didn't get a move on. You have a timing-device on your hands, E.

Kept hunching up, my neck was getting stiff.

The difficult supervisee was due at 9:50. I left a message, aware of a ratty stack of issues on the periphery, his whining and dependency, but for now—

Now I had to call him. From the international operator I got home, university and government numbers. Nearly ten—I'd wasted a lot of time. What if they quit at four there?

Caller hadn't said *when*.

I'd tell him what I had.

Negotiations, terrorists' demands, cease-fires: like games being played out on a vast field: I remembered living chess-games people used to play on college campuses. Strategies. Positioning.

Someone says the cease fire's at three, so at five minutes before, men are murdering each other, making young women widows and taking children's fathers, but five or seven or ten minutes later they sit out in the open having a cigaret, confident they won't be blown to pieces. I suppose if people running the wars considered the costs in particular and individual terms they'd have to quit.

I was helpless here.

Pay attention, Elena, I told myself; this is *interesting*. When I recovered from the fright and tension I'd have a lot to think about. Right now I was pressing buttons and holding the phone hard against my head. My hands hurt.

Finally—by now it was 10:15—I told his secretary I had a confidential message "from a friend" and that he must call me as soon as he possibly could, I would remain at this number. "If he rings and I don't answer I'll have gone for a bite of lunch, or to the bathroom…" I stopped. They don't say "bathroom."

She *knows* what one is. "I must speak to him as soon as possible." Then flaring with terror, "He's not out of the country, is he?"

"No, no," she said, "Not at all. I'm expecting him…"

If he were out of the country she probably wouldn't be permitted to say.

If he were out of the country, they would've known that. *They.*

This is completely unacceptable, I remember thinking.

"Well," I said finally, pleased with having thought it, "if it gets to be six o'clock here I'll have to go home." It'll be 11 p.m. there. This is absurd. "My number there is…"

I'd have to cancel everything—all my appointments, plans to talk with some of the children tonight.

My young client Jay was due at 11:15. It'd be easy to tell him there was an emergency I might have to deal with, he'd be fine with it. But the three people following him were dicier in various ways and I would be uncomfortable if we were interrupted.

I'd cancel. I was all hunched up and my neck was tight. It'd be better to have something to do, but how could I?

Cost me a day's wages, darlin', I told him in my head. Liam, where *are* you?

International intrigue. I remember thinking this—as a joke—with Liam in the hotel.

Someone had watched us.

Taken pictures?

This was at the edges of reason. Totally beyond. It wasn't about people; it was about nations and states. States of terror. I was getting nutso. Walking into the Crown I had thought a person could be looking out a window in the hotel across the street, the one we later went to and slept together in. Someone could've seen us. Could've filmed us.

Paranoia.

A bit of guilt operating.

More likely—I do remember thinking this—would be someone who knew him. A political enemy, or a friend, would call out Liam! I hadn't thought *surveillance*—who would?

Someone who knows who I am. Jesus.

And if I failed to get the message across seas and time? I saw the vast expanse of the North Atlantic deep gray and bottle-green and dotted with ice, miles-wide waves, little boats with men in yellow slickers, fishing vessels disappearing in the swells, tilting and bobbing.

The rain beat at the window and the phone didn't ring. My young client arrived, and I prepared him for an interruption which didn't come. I was able to focus on him but no sooner had he left than I was certain it'd been a mistake to cancel everybody else. My mind, untethered, soared off into a finely developed sequence of catastrophes.

I've had years of practice, with the children.

Let's be ordinary and unimaginative, E. There were an infinite number of possible minor glitches, missed elevators, flat tires, traffic accidents, bridges whose mechanisms had broken. When I was a kid we'd sometimes fake car-problems and stop all the traffic on the causeways from the keys back to the mainland. In the present in his country there could be army activity. A funeral. Any of these would keep him in his car, without privacy, and without my message. Why didn't I think of this? I should have told the secretary she had to reach him; surely she'd know how to find him.

You're out of your league, here, E.

No shit.

A man would've thought of this. A teenager who reads spy novels would've: cell phones with international SIM cards.

I couldn't be still, couldn't read. Drew cloud-shapes and circles. Without thinking, I filled pages with series of circles. Weren't there circles of stone in his country, old fortifications? It would be days before I remembered the sugar circle I'd made around his cup. Finally I sketched maps of his country and its surrounds. Then I added a list of place-names along the eastward edge, and it turned into a pleasing design. Maybe it'd be the cover of my next book. Terrific. *Drawn by the author while waiting to deliver terrorists' message to a statesman from X.*

My neck was stiff and throbbing and the phone stayed quiet. Maybe whoever saw me with him and called me was here, in the States, and had cut off my phone.

At last, at 1:03 p.m. (it said on the black and white digital clock on my desk, a present from Rory and Angela last year) the phone. My heart's rhythm jolted, hesitated, then ran. I felt it shift, like an old car. My voice tends to quaver when I'm stressed. I drew a breath, willing it crisp and level. "Dr. Elena Summerfield."

"It's me."

Tears filled my throat. "You're all right?"

"Oh aye," he said, hearty. "Sorry I wasn't able to return your call sooner."

"Oh, that's nothing." I replayed this brilliant response for days, an apogee of awkwardness.

"You took a call from a friend?"

"Oh yes, Liam. The man said, quote…" and told him.

"That's fine, then," said his statesman-voice, "Thanks very much."

I wanted to know how he was but wasn't sure how to ask. What was going on? I wanted something more from him.

"Good. Well, I just wanted to be sure you got the message." When he didn't speak I dared: "Tell me something local and specific."

"Let's see," I could hear warmth in his voice now. "Weather's ordin'ry, wind and rain."

I laughed.

"How are you?" He sounded as if he really wanted to know but then I imagined guys with reels of recording tape in a van somewhere—too much TV. I walked over to the window and looked down onto the street. "I don't know, frankly. Perhaps we'll talk another time, shall we?"

"That's a good idea. I'll telephone you next week."

"Call me at home," I said.

If something happens to him there won't be a next week.

I wanted to say *be careful* or *stay well*, but it wasn't possible.

I listened to the under-ocean cable tinging.

There isn't one. It's fiber-optics, inaudible. I imagined sounds of waves. It's all in your head, like sounds you hear in shells.

"Take care," I said finally, weak with my own incapacity.

"Yes indeed," he replied, blustery and professional, "You as well."

So much for the dramatic moment. I sat, shaking and suddenly very hungry.

The next morning I woke from dreams I hadn't called him, and the men kept telephoning, "You didn't do it. Why didn't you do what we asked you to?" Pretty obvious, the weight of responsibility.

I'm on another continent, I told myself, I've done what I could, which, as we know, is often not enough.

When you've had as many children as I have, your life is a continual lesson in how you can never do anything right, you're always responsible, inadequate, unsure.

How I got all those children is a story in itself and has also to do with violence on the periphery that became a determining element in my life.

It occurs to me that there are as many ways of murdering as there are of loving. Dear God!

For an unacceptably long time after the phone call, the telephone, that most banal of presences, jarred me. As if a reflex hammer tapped a bone, I'd become a flash of light. Then a week or ten days after the phone call to Liam I picked up a paper and there it was on the front page, dreaded and familiar: *Aide to Prime Minister Slain,* under a photo of a man in a suit crumpled on a sidewalk in front of what looked like 10 Downing Street but wasn't.

I knew immediately it wasn't Liam. Yet and still it's interesting how we do this: the evil averted, still we quake. I couldn't stop shaking.

It could have been. Of course it could. There are murders beyond counting, like the one that gave me my first children—a chance encounter, the brutal and unnecessary death. Choose any day at random: another bombing. Buildings, cars, truck-bombs, children murdered when their buses pass sentries in the Sinai Peninsula, in Georgia, Ukraine, Kabul, Northern

Ireland, Manchester, Delhi, Islamabad. Suicide-bombers, some of them women in chador. *Children.*

I want to scream.

It's the disease of our time—our primary random killer after cancer and AIDS—though thank God that's diminishing. Some days it exhausts me to know it's been going on all my life and will certainly go on after it.

Still, I was there, in Liam's country, and the picture of that man on the pavement terrified: it could have been Liam. It could have touched my life as that earlier murder had wrenched Terry's into undreamed-of forms.

And my own.

So here I am, a Jewish woman with five children named Summerfield and one named Weiss. Sometimes I can't believe it. Sometimes it makes me laugh.

When I married Terry Summerfield, my first love—it was mostly sex, of course, but he was older, he had lost his wife—he had the twins. They ran right into my heart past thinking, right into the maternal stuff waiting for a bit of moisture so it would flower. It certainly did that.

I think of her often—she's part of me now, through the children—how little and young she was, and how beyond comprehension her death. Her name was Phoebe, and she was Terry's wife. Before I was his wife, there was Phoebe, girl-mother of their twins— my children Bonita and Rory.

She was shot. Happened in a convenience store where she went to get milk while he was home with the sleeping babies. They were twenty-two months. So we had two children when we married, chose to have two, and then when my cousin Rachel died of cancer—her husband had MS and couldn't care for himself—we took her six-year-old, Flora. Then we chose to do it one more time. Why? God knows. We got Michael, now twenty-four. This meant we suddenly had six children. Not *suddenly*, but the recognition's sudden, because who has time when you're busy doing tons of laundry and incessant food-shopping and preparing and soothing and singing and bathing and negotiating and threatening ("If you let your sister have it for one day, you can have it for two…stop that fighting or you'll spend the day in your room!"), sprinkled in among the music lessons and car-pools and PTA meetings and recitals…

Well. With all of this going on you just aren't in the position to make intelligent decisions, and you're into sex in a big way because it's not childcare and it's soothing and you need to be an adult, so you don't think, and one day you wake up and oh my God: six children. How did this happen to us? Twelve children, when they marry, one of us said.

In bed one night, sitting and talking, my arms around my knees I remember, and Terry with a book in his hand. One of us said, What could we have been thinking? and we began to laugh. We rocked with laughter, howled with it, and then we cried and cried.

How can we have six children? How would there be any life at all for us with all these children? "Don't worry, sweetie," Terry said, "We can leave them in the park. And no breadcrumbs."

How would I ever have any time to myself, ever? How would I finish college and go to graduate school—a long dream?

When I look back on those years of exhaustion and tears and wonder, despite everything, I remember in my body the indescribable intensity and pleasure in my body, all of which seems to've been lived through by someone else, it's beyond comprehension. And I, a girl, was capable of years of patience and fury and devotion. Amazing. I do think humans were designed for devotion. It evolved as we did. And when the children began to need me less I chose a profession which required what I'd trained for.

At the time it was mindless, fecund, full of slick sex and salt and blood—we were like fucking rabbits. Completely in our bodies. Now I think it was just (*just?!*) nature working through us. And now I've traversed the line: the end is actually here. The too-familiar dryness. Sometimes I believe I can feel my uterus shriveling. I hate it so much I want to scream, but I'm a well-brought-up Southern lady and I never scream.

We used to wonder how we'd tell them, Terry and I. It turned out to be easy, natural—when they were very small we told them their momma had been hurt and the doctors couldn't make her better. When they were older, somehow it just emerged—after all that fuss and worry, I don't even remember how we did it. Strange what you remember. And what echoes. Last year—in January, freezing, major blizzard—I got a new client. Woman was the surviving child of a mass-murder: her father and mother and two sisters were killed by intruders. She was a baby, eight months old, asleep in her crib, and went unnoticed by the killers, who weren't caught for seven years. Her grandparents raised her and never told her what had happened to her family ("they died in an accident") until she'd finished college, four years before. They were getting old. They'd been afraid they'd die, and she would never forgive them for not telling her. "But how could they have?" she asked, reasonably.

I sat there stunned. A dozen questions sprang into my mouth: how could they protect you from this all those years? Did they raise you someplace else? What about your other set of grandparents, what about your parents' siblings? Right away I wanted William and his thoughtful responsiveness. As it was—as it is with most of life—I muddled through. "How long since they died?"

"Oh, my grandfather's still living. He's ninety-one," she grinned. "He's such a dear. He's all I have."

I am fifty-three years old and today I saw something I have never seen. It was merely our friendly old sun, but through clouds that blurred it entirely, so that the sun was a blare of light, a smear of brilliance in clouds that looked like clotted cream. At the edge, a coppery echo glowed, as if I were seeing its reflection—but on what? Another cloud, maybe. There it was, another sun, blue and copper, gleaming in the silver-white sky. I thought maybe it was a kind of rainbow I had never seen and how lucky I was to have had the moment—it was very brief, less than half a second; I was crossing the street, and then buildings blocked it, so I couldn't look long enough.

Metaphor for life, Elena, I told myself. The words *sun dog* came to me, but I don't know if that's what I saw.

Maybe it was because of all the children that we couldn't stay married, Terry and I. No leisure, no ease. Or: face it, Elena, I tell myself, you are not good at crowd control.

I was sixteen when Terry and Phoebe's twins were born. I married him—the young widower—when I was nineteen. This is not unusual if you come from where I did. Some of the girls I knew in junior high had children at fifteen. It will be obvious that I didn't have time for civil rights marches and things of that nature. During those hectic years I finished a bachelor's degree, in time stolen from my daily and not inconsiderable joy. And within a concentrated period they were all fledged, so when my youngest, Michael, was nearly twelve, I finally got to graduate school.

Terry and Phoebe had married at twenty-one because she was pregnant. Then they learned she was carrying twins. Uprushings of exaltation and terror and dismay and youthful pride—

Sometimes I wonder what their marriage would've been, had it a chance to get old. Sometimes I imagine those long-boned delicate lanky youngsters, Terry and Phoebe, in those days: he's in grad school at Tech, and they're both completely bewildered, but they love each other. They tell each other it'll be all right, they'll work it out, but the reality's concrete as a parking-deck: she's going to have *twins,* and they haven't any money and not much in the way of support from family—her people are older and not well and far away: they live in Grand Rapids, and his parents are in Toledo.

The children come. They are Rory and Bonita, who were nearly two when their mother died and not yet four when we married. We had Caroline and Sarah. Then Flora came to us. Michael.

For decades when I called one of them, the opening consonant stopped me. I stuttered and susurrated and spit. I laughed. They laughed. I cried. In those days I cried a lot. Pregnant with Michael all I could think was, we needed a very different kind of name for him. Flora was a near-rhyme with Rory, who had begged us for a brother, but he was just old enough to understand that we weren't entirely responsible for whomever we got. "We'll just love him—or her—to pieces," Terry used to say.

Rory never whined. Unlike Bonita. It's a gift to accept life as he does. So, we would hug him and tell him we'd do the best we could. When Michael arrived Terry sang out, we're evening things up! "It's way beyond this woman's capacity to *even things up*," I told him, and he kissed me and picked up the phone to tell the children. I wish we had planned that better. I wish he'd been able to take Rory aside and tell him himself, but Bonita answered, and he burst, "You have a new brother!" She shrieked. I heard her when he held the phone away from his ear, screaming, "It's a boy, Rory! Hey everybody, we got a brother-baby!" Great story for Michael, who's always enjoyed his special position, and whom everybody has loved without stint. It's amazing: none of the other children has ever tried to diminish him in any way. He shines. The family star, Bonita and Sarah call him. He's closest to Caroline, who was five when he was born, just old enough to hold him and push his stroller—as if she'd gotten a live doll of her very own. And Rory: I'll never forget the tremulous awe in his face when he first saw the baby. Bonita was thrilled, but Rory was—moved.

When I saw his face like that, I cried. I was full of milk and hormones and ready to cry at anything, but it was an astonishment. I cried for me and the new baby, I cried because of the children's welcome. And I cried for Rory, because of all that feeling. And for his mother, dead almost as long as his entire life. Sometimes that washes over me: she'd be forty, she'd be fifty-six. She'd be gray. Perhaps not. Perhaps, had she lived, she'd've been killed by a drunk driver at thirty-eight as she crossed an intersection. Perhaps anything.

We imagine life.

Phoebe remains a presence, a kind of beneficent shadow. I didn't know her but I have her children, so I know her in my body and my blood. She must've had a rough childhood with that name. I sometimes feel a wash of sorrow that she didn't get to watch those beautiful children grow up, and I did: accidental gift.

In all the photos she has long softly wavy sun-streaked honey-brown hair. She wore long flowery skirts and little white linen blouses she didn't iron.

She squints into the sun. In my favorite picture she's sitting on the grass—brightly green—and the twins, who are then about six months old, wave their arms and legs on a blanket before her. She's squinting but smiling at the same time, so her face is all screwed up, but it's so young and so lovely—as if she'll live a long time, grow old, have fat dimpled arms.

None of this will happen.

She will walk into Don's Convenience Corner one warm summer night after an exhausting but perfectly normal day taking care of her children, and she will get a loaf of brown bread with caraway seeds—they found it under her body—and a gallon of milk, which she will just have put down on the counter when the guy shot her. She hadn't turned around, hadn't known he was there, apparently. This is the only comfort possible. She had set it down and was probably getting bills out of her wallet.

Terry was working on his dissertation. He was at the typewriter in the dining area of the living room in their rented house when the doorbell rang. He thought he'd go help her bring in the groceries, she'd probably bought more than she'd intended and they'd be heavy, and there were the police.

His life slid away like the edge of a cliff breaking off, so that beneath the young husband, the father of two babies, there was nothing. He fell through early-evening air. He's said it was as if he were suddenly standing on water. Everything went fluid and he fell. He did fall. He wept and flailed and wept—for about three months, before he got hold of himself and picked up the remains of his life. Meanwhile his sister Arlette came to care for the children; she flew in from Poughkeepsie, where she was living with her husband, a foreman who worked construction, and stayed there, took a leave of absence from her job. He's said he never thanked her properly, though I don't know what kind of thanks would qualify, in the circumstances.

And she died, suddenly—lucky her—when we were married about four years. I liked her. She was a brusque woman who did actuarial work with a finance company, not warm or someone you could talk to, but the kind of woman who knew how to do what was needed without calling attention to herself. Occasionally I'd think we should have named Michael after her. I suggested it to Terry, but he didn't want to. It's always bothered me that what she had done for him and the children would die when we do. Jews believe that when you name someone for a person who has died it's a kind of immortality, so it was something I wanted, but it didn't have the same valence for Terry.

I couldn't put it away, though. It never quit troubling me that Arlette's name wouldn't live on, so I hired a lawyer—this was when Michael was seven and we lived in Rye—and went to court and changed his name from Michael Summerfield to Michael Arlet Summerfield, and I went home that night, and in the shower—the only place I was ever alone in those days—I told her. It wasn't enough, but it was all I could do.

Next day I picked Michael up at school. The children often told me their secrets in the car, on our way somewhere—so I couldn't react? I never thought that till now. We went for pizza, and I told Michael about his aunt, what-all she'd done for his daddy and his brother and sister and showed him her picture— "She looks like Daddy," he said. I told him I'd given him her name, and he would carry it, and she would live in his heart, and he should tell his children how he got his very special middle name.

Terry, scientist that he is, thought it unnecessary, but I was well pleased.

It hadn't worked so well when I'd tried something like it years before. Maybe we were just too raw in those days. I was pregnant with Caroline—my first pregnancy—and had gotten obsessed by the idea that Bonita and Rory wouldn't know their mother. It seemed a kind of crime. I probably felt guilty for the pleasure of their little arms around my neck, their little bodies against mine, their sweet, sweaty heads, all I had that she did not. I was, and remain, profoundly grateful to be part of the ongoing-ness of her children as well as the ones I gave birth to.

I made an enlargement of a photo of Phoebe—not my favorite, but one in which it was easy to read her features—and put it in the babies' room. "This is your birth-mother," I told them, but it confused them—I was their mother—and Terry couldn't stand to have it there. I wept many nights over my clumsiness and stupidity.

Good will counts for something, but not always.

There's nothing like child-rearing to make you feel absolutely inept and insufficient. On the other hand, driving a child home from the emergency room made me feel like the queen of competence.

I don't know how I did it. It was all accomplished through a fog of exhaustion, tears, and joy, milk dripping from my breasts and semen from between my legs.

One of the questions that remains vivid and present for me all these years on is how a girl becomes a woman. I did it, but I don't understand the transformations age and hormones and experience— and love—bring with it. It's incomprehensible. I know. I keep saying that—I asked Gaynell once, how did I go from a being girl who was interested in boys and clothes to a woman who's a therapist interested in social issues and political change and class? When did I start looking at men with gray hair?

She laughed really hard that time, did Gaynell

Much later, in training, I learn I'm (nominally) in charge of what's called a "blended" family. Makes me think of butter and sugar and flour in one of those mammoth yellow ceramic bowls too heavy to lift.

"Mums," the voice on the answering machine says, "call me ASAP."

FYI, ASAP. My only comfort is they're fads and will disappear.

Flora, whom I call by many love-names, Flor, La Fleur, White Flower—which is in fact her name, Flora Weiss, my cousin Rachel's daughter who came to me when she was six, has been my child ever since.

I call. "Guess what? New job! Internal," she adds. I don't know whether this is good or not. She's been interviewing both with her own company, an ad agency, and others. She's been in a cubby off someone's office, which though she's in New York means she might as well be in Turkmenistan, she says.

"Things aren't good for women in Turkmenistan," I said.

"Whereas here in Nueva York," she cracked, "everything's cool."

"Where?"

"Chicago."

I hope she doesn't hear my exhalation of relief. "And?"

"I have three weeks to bop over there and back to do office and housing."

"Great! Great. Have you called Michael?" He's in grad school in Chicago. "He'll help you look."

"Just got off the phone with him." She sounds wonderful.

"Terry and I lived there when we were first married," I said, which of course she knew.

When she came to us she called me Cousin Elena, which over time elided to Cousin'lena—"Sounds like a Finnish city," Terry joked; he'd been to a conference at Suomenlinna. Then, tentatively, in her early teens, Mumsie and Mums. Throughout, Terry remained Terry, or Cousin Ter. "Kid has a gift for shortening things," he said once. Terry had—has—a pleasing dry wit, very male, I think of it as. Sometimes the boys come out with something like that and I have to pull myself up: why am I surprised? They're his children too.

We were in Chicago for Terry's post-doc. It's the chapter in my life called Southern Girl Meets Winter. Rained ice-water. Froze my *eyes.*

Like to froze my soul. It was gray for weeks at a time, and I was stuck indoors with Bonita and Rory. I couldn't realize it then because my own new life was overwhelming, but my young husband was living in a maelstrom: grief which was beginning to fade, but which erupted in caught breath and bad dreams, and longings. I can't imagine. And he was dealing with the requirements of a new wife and a demanding young family—twin children, their needs immediate and unremitting. He was in an unfamiliar professional setting with new colleagues, some of whom he would have to learn to trust—which ones?—and working in exacting research.

Sex saved us, probably. It was the only thing we both wanted, apart from the babies, who were little wild things, convulsing us with laughter and tears. "Wild baby animals," Terry said once, his eyes filling. Years of this—maybe three to five. And as for me, I'd been caught up—think fish flopping in a great net in the warm blue waters somewhere between Cuba and Tampa—and dropped into a bay off Newfoundland. With glaciers.

And poor Terry, who'd been shattered. I both knew it and couldn't know the soul-scourging depth of how it was for him.

For many years Phoebe remained present—to both of us. She was there, a presence in the middle of it all. Not a negative—nor a benign—presence, and not a ghost. She was a *person* we both loved. She belonged to me too, because she had left me her children.

Our days were completely heroic. *Typo!* Hectic, I meant to say. Both true.

With the babies we had no time for our own lives, and yet that was what our lives were made of. While all that was foregrounded, in the background—where we were too tired to notice—our own development was going on.

I thought I would die there.

The snow, driven horizontal by unstopping winds, terrified me. I woke up sometimes from my inadequate sleep—by then I was pregnant—into whirls of white and the wind blowing and clattering, the sky like cement.

When it got nice I took the children to the lake, and I liked it there, but it was a poor substitute for my Gulf, warm and easy. I started buying gardenias in the winter during those two years in Chicago. Then we came back to the East Coast, to Rye, and made a suburban life there, and got Flora-lora-lora.

"When do I get to take you out to dinner to celebrate?" I asked her now.

"Anytime! And the days before I leave. When I'll need it."

If Flora's father hadn't lived till she was twelve we probably would've adopted her and given her the last name all the other children have, but it would've felt to him like a hastening. And then of course it wasn't possible to offer it.

Flora-belle, I used to call her, and Flora-lee.

Child of Rachel, who died, leaving me her daughter.

Flora's much taller than I, tall as her mother was. "You're so little!" she used to chortle when she grew. I would draw myself to my full height—five one-and-a-half, but she and Rachel are and were five seven—giants. Rachel was my age-mate and, history being less imaginative than God, my mother had raised her, because *her* mother died when she was a girl.

Not of the cancer that twenty years later would kill her daughter. She took her own life, leaving Rachel at five. Sometimes in dreams I hear my great-aunt Sarah calling, *Ray-chel! Rayyy-chel!* We were five months apart, so we became sisters. The sorrow went underground. I was a child, thrilled to get another sister of my very own.

Losing her was terrible.

Flora looks just like her mother. I love looking at her; she's so *big,* so fleshy. Even to myself I don't know how to say it. She's like a gardenia-petal, white, thick-fleshed, and beautiful. Absolutely. She has masses— *yards!* -- —of curly jet hair and sparkly brown eyes. My sisters and I are small and round: face, eyes, mouth. My sisters' hair is brown with no hint of red, and they have golden eyes. Consequently people think we do not look alike. We do, in the red (me) or honey (them) versions.

Rachel, however, was not only tall but very slim and lean, with fine Arab-looking lips (*What does that mean?!* I shrieked at her description one day. *Carved,* she said. *Articulated. Oh, carved.*). Mine are more like a fat pout.

Ahhh, the faces of our dearly loved…

Once I saw her dead mother's face in Bonita. She was five. She had slipped in a puddle the dog made on the kitchen floor, and, highly insulted, screwed up her little face and wailed. I lifted her—we'd both have to have baths to get the stinky urine off—and held her close, my face against her little fat cheek. I'd done this countless times, but this time I saw Phoebe. I remember weeping as I carried her upstairs. "How would you like to have a shower with me?" I asked, because now she was crying hard, frightened by my intensity.

"Shower!" A major treat. I carried her into our bathroom—Terry and I had a stall shower off our bedroom, which for me, a girl raised without extras and the mother of a veritable mob, was the ultimate luxury. "Rory," I called, "Stay absolutely where you are, all right?"

"I want a shower too!"

"Come on, then!"

I stripped off our clothes and left them in a heap right there on the bathroom tiles. Rory hopped around, wild with impatience while Bonita leaned into the falling water, laughing while I adjusted the flow. I put her down and pulled his clothes off too and we scrubbed and shampooed and laughed and sang. It was ten o'clock in the morning, and when I got out of there, I'd have to wash the kitchen floor and deal with the dog, but right then, under the warm spray with Phoebe's son and daughter, I had a moment of perfection. Now and then I've seen a flicker of her mother, but never again with the clarity of that day. I suppose Bonita's personality has modified whatever she's inherited of her mother's face.

The Summerfield Family at Home

(a story I seem to need to write but will never publish)

Caroline is in the family room planning some festivity or other; she's the Social Dictator, her father says—forever organizing plays and games, bringing friends home to sprawl in the big family room off the kitchen. Why did we call it that? All the rooms were family rooms. She's fourteen. I'm gathering materials—finally—to go to grad school. We live in a big Victorian house in Rye, because Terry's director and vice president of Alpha-Tech, a company that develops polymers for industry. It's an R&D firm and he's making tons of money, but it doesn't feel like it, because of all those children. Caroline's studying painting and will eventually go to art school and Paris (decades late, I do not say) and Rome. I guess it's never too late for Rome—or Paris.

She has just set the table; next week it's Sarah's turn; there's a calendar on the back of the door of the broom-closet. Mary, the cleaning-help, has been in today, so it must be a Thursday. Michael would have been nine then, and coming in sweaty from play—it's a spring evening -- late April. The ground's muddy but things are beginning to bloom. The white dogwood outside the dining room windows is about to burst into flower, and that very morning I have noted fat pink buds out my bedroom window on the crab-apple. We have lilacs in the back where Terry wants to build a gazebo. I think it's a waste of money. What I most want is a second-floor deck: it'll feel like floating. Tonight the children will help us decide. That's the plan.

What happens instead is, Sarah, running around the corner of the house, snags her foot on a root and, because of the momentum, throws her body hard against the edge of the handrail at the side steps. "Attacked by my own house!" she'll say for years. She tears a deep gouge in the flesh of her upper arm and there are buckets of blood. Everybody's screaming. I grab a bunch of dish-towels and run, slipping in the mud myself.

Apply pressure. I hug her hard, the towels between us. But I'll have to let go to drive, because Terry's not home. "Get me a belt," I yell to Michael, watching, pale and shaken.

Rory and Bonita are away at school. Flora's on a trip to Milan and Florence. Why? Why not. She has dropped out of school twice, it will take her eight years to do a college degree—but she will have had a great time and learned a lot of wonderful things instead of being stuck in a library.

Michael sprints off. Late that night I'll find the ridge of mud from his shoes where he rounded a corner upstairs. He and Caroline forgot to clean there when they tried to put everything back. Using the belt as a kind of body-tourniquet, I strap Sarah into a hunch, the towels pressed against her arm, get her into the car and drive to the hospital. She's dead-white by then, a terrible color, and streaked with sweat and dirt from where she'd been wiping away tears with a dirty hand.

I no longer remember how many times I was in that emergency room. I remember Michael with a scalp wound and assorted sprains after hours, Rory with a greenstick fracture of one of the long bones in his right arm. I'd have to ask. Things I thought I could never forget have melted away. Flora with a broken fourth finger, Sarah with a wrenched neck from a fall off a jungle-gym which would lead to a year of headaches. I remember Bonita with a rattle in her chest once and a violent rash another time, and once a broken collarbone. Rashes scared me, because I imagined them intractable, spreading to all my children, searing their soft skin, and scarring.

Caroline, thank God, nothing. She's very careful, typical of her place in the (second) family. I remember taking her for her first bra, showing her how to fit it properly and wear it, her little face all twisted, grumbling, "Boy, there sure are a lot of *parts* you have to take care of." Little do you know, my girl, I did not say.

That time was—in fact—another life, a life in which one of the principals was someone who looked and sounded a lot like me but wasn't. How could it possibly have been?

I have noticed that mothers disappear. Both before and after they have died. How can it be that the most perfect love I have experienced, that mindless animal-summoning self-obliterating love, has faded until it's almost memory instead of act, and that men I have loved have moved into the foreground, bright and requiring and consuming? The children have gone off into the complex landscapes they create as they stride forward, step after long step with someone they love, or a series of someones. Or toward something.

My whole life altered while I was living it. And now as if I'm standing in a brief clearing, echoing with loss, it's as if all those years I hadn't been paying attention—

I met Toss Ando, born Tomás Ando in Durban, South Africa, of Korean parents, at a party given by Dan, who was then a new friend and colleague. Toss had come with a tall Asian woman and I noticed that his eyes twinkled. Like Ciro and like Liam he's charming. Women fall for him. I was one in a long series.

Makes me squirm.

"Toss," he said, holding out a compact brown hand, which I shook. It was soft and very strong, a hand that hasn't done outdoor work, I thought, but I was wrong; he was a sculptor and was taken by my coloring, he said later. Asking what I did, and without my being aware of it, drew me away from the others toward the corner, sat on the floor, and pulled me into a chair. "Come, sit down, tell me where you got that glorious hair. Tell me what you do. Tell me your name."

I write this feeling like a naïf. Truth is, I am naïve, an unseemly quality for a New York professional woman of some capacity but there it is. Bizarre unfitting parts flourish without our approval. I know this because it's my business to know it. As if our psychic lives were Miró paintings, all those unexpected little yellow blobs and squiggles of red or black coming into view.

Toss didn't care if I was married, but I did. I had a commitment to my marriage and all those children. Michael was eighteen and though I was at the end of the child-years, it's a cast of mind—I know now—that will never leave me. I'd been in school since he was twelve and that was the year I would finish my degree and leave my husband of twenty-five years, but at the time I didn't know any of this.

I can't say—even to myself—what it was like. It was like everything, like a log being slipped into a stream, the initial slow movement barely perceptible. But then most of it is in the water and floats free. Not without a lot of suffering as it knocks this way and that, moving downstream with the current, picking up speed as it gains momentum. That's what happened to us, to Terry and me, and at the same time we had an intensely civil and thoughtful marriage, with each of us caring a great deal about the other's well-being. How could we leave such a thing -- a thing we had made?"

I don't know.

It was over, it fell of its own weight, a shelf of snow off a limb, an organic growing thing. Perhaps as it grows wind or subtle movement loosens the bottom layer and opens a space between snow and branch, an infinitesimal space, and milder air, or an uprush of fluids in spring heats the branch a bit, then *plop!* the snows shift and fall, the branch is naked.

Too many elements. I write short stories so I know there's supposed to be one overarching metaphor, but it was my *marriage.* My life.

Twenty-four hours a day all through the years of my young womanhood and into middle-age. Awful. But old age will be worse, so chill, E, I tell myself— vainly.

As for the harmonies that evening, Toss took my hand and talked with such marvelous intensity— intensity which was just simply not in Terry's nature— I didn't take it seriously. Two weeks later he called, and I was astonished. What could he possibly want? Me. A rush of delight, like sudden sunlight after a squall. The squall was probably my squalid household. It wasn't squalid, of course, but everywhere there was dog-food and soggy cereal and pieces of half-eaten fruit and dirty socks and odd sneakers and endless need and laundry, and no matter how often I shopped, a permanent need for food.

At the time, taking Toss surprised me. Not only was I married and not consciously thinking of leaving Terry, but an affair didn't fit my self-picture. I was a faithful wife, a good woman. "Enough of that, eh?" I remember Gaynell saying.

"Conscience."

She laughed.

I hadn't thought I was into risk, as for example Ciro is, with the sky-diving and light planes and playing the market.

It was clear during Toss's phone call what the visit would be about. I don't know how I realized this, but I knew it, and I went into town on the train feeling shy and giddy, like a girl with a secret, effervescence and delight threatening to burst right out into public laughter.

Ah, Toss.

We'd lie in his bed in his studio near the East River— if my momma could've seen what I'd had to walk over to get there, she would've purely died. I remember most vividly the clean fury of his entering me, and after, when we'd talk. He'd stroke my back and hip, my hair. I'd lie facing him, feeling his sex soft against me. We were damp and quiet and his hand moved almost absently. "I think my parents passed," he said once, almost as if he weren't aware of speaking out loud.

"Passed," I echoed, burying my face in his chest, thick and soft and not too furry. I like men with substantial bodies and not a lot of hair.

"In South Africa in those days Japanese were honorary whites."

"Jesus," I exclaimed, pulling back to look at him. "Are you serious?"

"Outrageous, isn't it?" he said without energy. "So I believe they made as if they were Japanese, to the authorities."

That must've been more of a shame than passing for white, I thought, as he said "We had Korean friends, went to a Korean church…"

"Didn't they keep track of who went where?"

"I expect they were busy enough with the blacks."

I remembered having read something—couldn't remember what—about Japanese mistreatment of Koreans.

What must it have cost his family to do this?

He had a wonderful accent. Southern Hemisphere, with some of the distinctive sounds of English spoken in New Zealand and Australia, Southern Africa. For yes, *yeys.*

Take me home, I thought. "Imagine coming from there."

He chuckled. "It's about as exotic as Salt Lake City. Or Shanghai."

"I knew a Jew," I told him, "who grew up there. To escape the Germans some Polish Jews went east, spent part of the war in Shanghai."

"Speaking Polish throughout," he said.

"Tell me about Durban."

"Mostly Muslim. Very steamy. Like where you're from."

"That's why I want to see it."

He told me something of the city's spicy smells, the morning and evening sun on it. "If I got off a plane in the middle of the night blindfolded I'd know Durban from the smells."

"Can you see Madagascar from the beach?"

He laughed and laughed. Kindly, sweetly, rocking me, and laughing.

"What?"

"It's two-hundred-fifty miles offshore. And north. East of Mozambique. It's huge, Elena, fourth-largest island in the world."

"Americans don't know geography," I told him. "We learn our own neighborhoods. Once on the way back from Sweden there was a TV screen on the seatback in front of me, and when the image of the little plane flew into the mouth of the St. Lawrence, I felt, absurdly, that I was home. I knew where I was on the grid we've thrown over the world. We'll never comprehend it—"

Dear Toss. Sometimes it comes to me, unbidden, the curve of his brown cheek.

I would have thought, I told him, that his work would reflect the part of the world he came from, but it was so abstract I couldn't see any Southernness in it. "Universal language," he said.

"I thought that was music."

He got up and put on a CD of South African music, very low and beautiful, the drums like heartbeat.

Even fast and irregular, their beat was human scale, nothing so declarative as rap.

"Drums don't translate well," I said, sitting up on the bed, the black-and-red plaid cotton blanket around me, while he padded around putting water on for coffee, setting out his turquoise Fiestaware plates on a black cloth with brown zebra-stripes. Really ugly combination, I thought, But what do I know?

He grinned. "Sometimes I think rap's very Western," he said, "Aggressive. Like Western politics: we're going to rule the world."

"Yeah," I said. "I hadn't thought—I do know I can't stand it."

"These guys're singing in Zulu," he said.

"Can you speak it?"

"Everybody there speaks it."

"Tell me some."

It sounded like an Asian language, very soft and nasal and full of breath.

"And you said…?"

"Goodbye," he laughed.

"That's all?!"

"No." He grinned. "I said you are a beautiful woman, Elena."

I gasped. How could I be beautiful? This ordinary body, maker of babies. Lover of—now—men, plural. *Beautiful?* Sturdy, yes. Efficient. Flawed. I shrugged, laughing, and hugged the words. Nothing remarkable here, I thought, Except maybe the hair.

I watched his brown muscular body move with what I think of as that complete male unselfconsciousness. I was forty-four, sexually knowledgeable, but unable to be comfortable naked with a strange man. Even then I knew I'd chosen Terry for his powerful sexuality and need. His need for me, and for his babies. My need for children. I moved into being their mother with such immediacy that I no longer remember, nor can I separate, Terry-and-me from Terry-and-the-children-and-me. All of that kept the marriage going longer than it might have.

And then I chose Toss for the same reason, assuring myself it was something else. It appeared to be something else, but it was need. The same string, struck, yields my note.

In training I began to think Toss represented— was—a precious gift, something mine alone, a dimension of my life that didn't touch my marriage.

Which was of course not possible.

What kind of shrink keeps saying, about men, that she doesn't know why she left this one, chose that one?

Liam and Ciro too. Sex cloaked in some other combination of appealing male attributes: power, upper-body strength. Lower-body silkiness and delicacy and solidity. Mindless animal authority. Who knows what it is.

And of course brains and wit and nice hands and pretty mouths and watchful eyes. Intensity. Men to whom I didn't have to explain. Their ability to learn me. And except for my husband, none of them American—Ciro only technically.

How absolutely strange.

Sex and its variant requirements, its continual surprise. Once I remember rising from Toss's bed thinking It's always singular and always the same.

I did an extraordinary thing with Toss. It was so unlike me, and so perfectly suited me, it chokes me when it rises into consciousness all these years later, and it's related to something quite strange and terrible I learned about myself.

I don't know I'm in an emergency until afterward. So when the men said, "We know you know Liam," perhaps for the first time in my life I knew—but not in words: this is an emergency.

How can it be that someone's life is in jeopardy and she doesn't know it?

One doesn't dramatize: it's tasteless. I learned that early, and never knew I'd learned it.

In some schools of psychology everything's your fault. Even disease. Outrageous.

The emblematic event actually had nothing to do with me. It was the Avianca flight inbound to New York. Avianca says, we're running low on fuel. English is not his native language, and he does not say, this is an emergency. The tower says, we'll bring you around one more time, and routes them out over the ocean.

They all died.

I had to learn to say *this is an emergency* to myself so that I could say it to others, and then when I got the call about Liam there wasn't anybody to say it to.

Life-threatening means not figuratively. In some sense when I left Terry it was actual, if not material. I mean to say it was not visible, but it was a consuming pain; suffering. A word I hate to use because I have two legs and can walk; I'm not dying of some terrible disease—that I know of. The pain was constant and at the same time my ordinary life went on…life went on…and we were courteous and thoughtful and talked in quite civil ways to one another, while I was shriveling up inside. And at the same time—oddly— growing in capacity for freedom, in some profound way that I knew and couldn't articulate. Something new was required. Not new as in novelty, but something insubstantial and entirely other. Some other self, some other way of being.

Like caterpillar to butterfly—or moth—changing form absolutely—and yet related to the prior life- form. No wonder I can't find words for this—

All my life I was responsible for them, those squirmy delicious sweating waste-producing little human animals (laughing as I write this) who'd someday, now, be grownups, people who drive cars and go wherever they like on their own, accomplished people who love and fret and do things. Terry wasn't terribly involved with them in the daily, but I know they are buoyed up by his love for them, and if they ask, he's available. He never said I'm busy, though he was gone most of the time, studying, doing his work.

My work was the children. And Terry. So when I left him it was a relief because, the children fledged, for the first time since I was nineteen I didn't have to take care of anybody—except of course I went into a field that's all about taking care. But finally it's framed, limited, clearer, and not—thank God!—permanent.

How it ended. Toss and I met in a hotel room. He was preparing his studio for a weekend of tours and interviews—*Meet the Artist on His / Her Own Turf*—designed to raise money for artists with AIDS.

For this encounter, I bought navy silk underthings. What possessed me? Perhaps the affair with Toss was a repudiation of the ordinariness, an ordinariness that had stunted something in me, some wild-girl thing my early marriage prevented me from experiencing. The affair, like grad school and training, revivified me. I understood that I'd been stunned—as if I'd taken a blow to the head.

Perhaps—this is ugly—I didn't need him anymore, dear Toss. I wasn't conscious that this would be the last time, but I think now I must've bought the underwear to mark it.

Gorgeous and extravagant handmade navy silk underwear. I got there before he did and changed in the hotel room.

When it was over, I made him leave first.

I stood weeping in the strange room with its thick draperies and almost-invisible stripes on the wallpaper.

On the heavy door to the bathroom, an old-fashioned beveled mirror showed my reflection. I do believe I watched myself do it, as one would watch a movie. I balled up the silk underthings and dropped them into the wastepaper basket.

I'd enacted it: it was over.

I got back into my gray wool dress over plain nylon underwear and walked out of there, and out of Toss's life.

For days and days—maybe even months—afterward, I heard a refrain in my head, like a song: *You will die, you will die, You will die.*

I thought it was guilt, probably, but whatever it was, it told me how hard my having done it—and losing it—was. And then one day, it said *You will find,* but I heard it once only, and consider it an aberration.

The family systems people would say—and I agree—that I needed something of my own in that household where there were all those children, all that noise, demands, all that sticky fusion. There were no spaces shaped like me.

Terry is a long slender man, angular, with light hair and light freckled skin, unlike Toss, who was in many ways a prefiguring (or echo) of Ciro.

I'd thought I could keep the affair with Toss fenced in. I would make certain it didn't touch the other parts of my life, but in spite of my best efforts it came to mean too much. For a while it meant everything.

Then it no longer did.

What happens to consuming passion six months later? To obsession? Once a client said, "I was totally obsessed with him for...for half an hour, maybe forty-five minutes," and was surprised when I laughed and laughed.

People know things that aren't good for them and permit them to go on. I think Terry must've known the red coals at the center of our marriage were going cold. Perhaps he didn't believe his instincts. Perhaps he was worn out with trying. Perhaps—the simplest answer is often best—perhaps he simply could not imagine what to do. And I? What did I do? The unkindest answer is: run for my life.

On the other hand, I was so busy, so taken up, I didn't imagine large-scale repercussions. Stupid, that was.

And for his part, Toss hadn't required or importuned. He'd invited me, and I'd walked into the affair as easily as I walk into the Gulf at home. And when it was over he seemed to understand without much information. Or he was sensitive to information I hadn't known I had, as animals sense the ground about to tremble before an earthquake.

One of the remarkable things about us—human critters—is how much information we have, and use, mindlessly. Toss took me once—where was Terry? How did I manage to get away? Where were the children?

Toss took me to a crummy little house he had in a village up along the Hudson, not far from Bear Mountain. It was very beautiful as we drove up along the river, villages and dense forests, and as we got farther north, impenetrable swaths of evergreens, lakes and lots of granite. At his little brown bungalow, a really dingy poor affair such as I'd've grown up in, had I been raised Upstate, he showed me his garden and, as he drew me along, I realized I was resisting going into it. It was so shabby and tentative. "It's scary," I said, and he stopped and looked at me, waiting.

"Ghosts?" he asked, amused, his face tilted upward, all the planes of it beautiful in the clear north light.

"It looks so—poor," I said.

"It's just a cabin," he replied, unoffended. "A studio. I do some work here. Not a lot. Come in. You'll be surprised. You'll like it."

He was right: inside, pure surprise, all white and open, with bright red and sea-blue cushions here and there, and a massive yellow lampshade dangling from the ceiling like a beach umbrella. I laughed.

"See?" he asked and pulled me into a kiss.

Then he said "Now the real surprise. You have to come upstairs. It's where I keep the poltergeists," he added, straight-faced.

"Toss—"

"C'mon," he said, and pulled my arm like a kid urging me into a hiding place.

I followed him up the dark wooden steps, our footfall echoing. The house had a nice woody smell, and a big square window on the landing. Broad leaves filled it. Oak? I wish I knew the names of northern trees.

Upstairs we went into the bedroom where a futon lay on the floor covered in one of his ghastly African print things, black and yellow zebra-striped with red and green trim, and words on it. "Swahili," he said, watching my eye.

"Kenya?"

"Tanzania. But look, this is what I wanted you to see," he said drawing me to the window, which turned out to be a door, which he flung open onto a wide second-story deck floating in the trees.

"Oh, this is *wonderful.*" I went to the edge of it and leaned on the railing. It was maybe only twenty-feet up, but it was off the ground: "I absolutely love it," I said, going to him. "What do you do out here?"

"We shall see, my dear." He leered comically.

"I have to go home," I told him, laughing.

"But you'll want to come back," he said. I always did want to, and never did. It has haunted me since, that porch in the sky. Sometimes when I'm having trouble falling asleep, solving problems instead of letting down into rest, I think of it: I imagine the whole structure swinging a bit in a light breeze, and if I were sleeping out there, the wind like water moving all over me.

But the point was, he made it. "Built it in one weekend," he said.

I gaped. "By yourself?"

"I had to have some help. Beams're heavy."

"It only took you one weekend?"

"Well, I planned it. Took a couple of evenings." He grinned. "Had to order the materials. That took some time."

On the way back I said, "Don't you think it's astonishing that you could just build that deck in one weekend?"

"Why would I?"

"I could never in a million years. Even with plans," I said.

"But you can cook a seven-course dinner. You know how to do that."

"Gendered information."

"Right." I remember he patted my thigh.

A long while after it ended, two or more years it was, I saw him on a street in SoHo and we hugged and went for a drink and talked, and then we were in touch, with a kind of erratic regularity, until he died.

Shocking language: *he died.* Or the monumental: *my mother died.* It simply does not weigh anything: you want to say *the* world *has ended,* but you say *my mother died,* and sometimes your eyes water. The language is so bizarre: *he died.* As if it were a choice. It's a passive verb in active form. Or it's active but we understand it as passive.

Even *I left my husband* has none of the power of the reality.

Knowing this has helped me listen in my work. Charles always understood this, and he helped me to learn it in ways I try to hand along to the people I supervise: a quality of attention unlike any I've experienced. Charles. Not a day passes that I do not send loving thanks his way.

In the early years of my marriage it is well before Toss. I have not imagined my future because I am so tangled (stuck?) in the present. (I can say "stuck" now but I wasn't aware of being stuck then: I was madly in love with the children and my life.) I am too busy to remember that I have an imagination, that one day I will be a woman; I'm a girl still. Terry and I have been married two years. The twins are nearly five and I am pregnant with Caroline, and we are going to Toledo, to Terry's people, for Thanksgiving.

They are perfect dumplings, the children: Rory has round brown eyes and tatty brown hair—he loves having it shaggy, and is constantly picking it up with his hands, leaving it standing this way and that. "Horns," he declared once, which Terry and I repeated occasionally for years, smoothing his hair. Bonita is quieter than her brother, a happy child with a ready smile. She has the same eyes in a very different face: it's more like her mother's, with brown hair she loves to wear in "bunches," one on each side of her head. She likes colored bows in them and lets me fuss with her hair, a perfect daughter.

Always my images of Terry have children in them, though at the same time he's never home—very weird. In the images when he is home, the children scamper around him, hang from his shoulders and long legs and ride on his back and curl around his body in his special inner-tube hold. In my recollections when he's home they're always laughing.

All through those years I read the paper (or read *in* the paper) a few times a week and looked at the headlines daily. In the periphery of our lives, there are all sorts of terrorism and brutality and violence. I notice this and do not notice it; it gave me Bonita and Rory, but until the message to Liam it never occurs to me that it could happen to me.

La Isla

In September Ciro called to say he was going to Boston on business, so I flew up to meet him.

I had a friend in Cambridge, I told him and "My son Rory lives there with his wife." I described my new daughter-in-law Angela, a beautiful young woman nearly as tall as Rory—a classical music radio disc-jockey—with long thick golden-brown hair I covet because it's nearly straight.

Then I called my old grad school friend Chet and arranged to meet him for lunch. Good talk followed by a lovely afternoon meandering through the Coop and little shops, where I picked up a handsome little pitcher for Rory and Angela, in case I saw them. At five I took a cab back into Boston to meet Ciro at the Copley Plaza for dinner.

Winging it, I told myself, thinking it'd be good for me to try out a new behavior: if he didn't invite me, I'd take a hotel room and call the kids. If he did, I'd stay with him and try to see them in the morning. Or—this felt absurdly illicit—fly home without telling them.

Dinner was what dinner would have been if I had married him: elegant, rich, and expensive, and—uncomfortable to acknowledge—boring. He talked about property and investments and stocks and strategies. It was astonishing: he didn't ask me one thing about myself or my life. I could have been a witch-doctor for all he knew.

"He must've talked about politics," Gaynell said, when I told her.

"No," I said, thinking. "Now that's really interesting, 'cause it's what he does. Why does he not, d'you suppose?"

"Crooked deals," she suggested, serious.

I gave her a look.

"Cubans don't let anybody in, Gringa."

"Gaynell, that is evil." I laughed. She's Cajun, with, as she puts it, who knows what-all blood. She's tiny and very dark, with that wonderful thick straight black hair. Striking, I told her once, a long time ago.

"Don't you have to be tall to be striking?" I remember this because it broke something loose in us, and I think marked the beginning of our friendship.

Gaynell and I: girls together, and women.

"D'you think he didn't talk to you because he's on guard?"

"He did talk to me."

"About himself," she said with emphasis.

"Doubtless."

"Doubtless," she echoed. Long ago we'd agreed that nothing was doubtless. Her grand-aunt—the only family she has left—had gone to see that movie, *Mrs. Doubtfire,* and called it *Mrs. Doubt-free,* which Gaynell could simply not get over.

But that night with Ciro, as I sat listening, what I had thought quite clearly was, I am being excluded from this conversation. It wasn't a conversation, it was a lecture.

Instead of getting angry I'd found myself amused, and despite everything, comforted by his presence. Which is really odd.

When he didn't invite me to join him, but got ready to put me in a cab to wherever I was going -- I had to think of someplace—"Just let me check," I said, going to use the cellphone in the women's lounge while Ciro waited in the lobby.

Men waiting while I've used the rest room or made a phone call or bought something in a store: why does this fascinate me? Because mostly they don't? Face it, E, I thought sharply: you make sure it isn't necessary. I sighed. There's still a lot of nice little don't-make-waves Southern gal under all the acquired educational cladding. I laughed aloud: *cladding.*

"Rory? I'm in town. Is it too late to crash on your sofa?"

"Mom, great!" My heart lifted.

"I'm having dinner with a friend. I'll take a cab…" He wouldn't hear of it. So then Ciro and I waited; it was a kind of role reversal, as if we couldn't drive and were waiting for one of our parents to bring us home from a dance. We sat in leather club chairs in the lobby and I told him a bit about how I came to be Rory and Bonita's mother. "I'm a lucky woman," I said, "to have so many children." I wanted him to have some sense of the dizzying collage my life has been: my four little girls like unkempt dolls, stringy hair flying, whirling and skipping and leaping, concentrated little faces fixed in attitudes of difficulty and delight in dance contests and shows and plays with curtains made from old sheets and towels, sofa cushions carefully arranged and pulled apart so we could see "the stage." His daughter had died. I couldn't possibly tell him this.

Rory strode in, tall and fair and lanky, like his father. Hugs and laughter. When I turned to introduce Ciro I was struck by how much shorter and darker and older he looked as he shook hands with my son. Ciro and I did a public mostly-air kiss and I left with Rory.

"Who's the guy?"

"I've told you about Ciro; he drew my father's will."

It was enough. We drove to his apartment where Angela, in a green silk caftan, her skin glowing, had tea and coffee-cake waiting. "What a darling!" We visited awhile, and Rory gave me a tour of the photographs they had up everywhere. I especially liked the ones on ledges Rory'd built along two of the dining-area walls. He'd been trying to show his work here and there, and they talked about that. Angela knew a lot of people in the Boston arts scene and was sure he was on the verge of recognition.

She had gotten interested in journalism, she said, and would be taking a course in January. I loved it: it gave me energy, all their youth and enthusiasm and hard work.

They went to bed, leaving me in the living room in a sweatshirt Rory'd given me, saying "The heat's not very good in here."

All the children continue to amaze in their autonomy and maturity. No matter how often I think it, I'm astonished: a baby I'd held in my arms, whom I'd loved with mindless purity, has become this unknowable person, a man, a grown-up son. Accomplished in countless ways, with a world of inner—and outer—experience. Somebody's *husband.*—Then, thinking about Ciro, I understood. He hadn't invited me because he had someone. Of course. And weirdly scrupulous for a man who'd had a lot of women.

Why had I never considered marrying him? Every time I ask myself this question I come up with a different answer, and some of them have to do with his being first-generation. There weren't a lot of educated Cubans in Sarasota then—probably still aren't. It wasn't till nearly the mid-sixties when Castro's hold on power had grown more solid and unmistakable that people began to emigrate in large numbers—and they went, as everybody knows, to Miami, the educated and the rich. Which was significant, because the rich hadn't needed to leave before Castro. Since the late 1800s, poor people had always somehow made their way across the Straits.

I can see his mother: she was a beautiful woman, elegant, buxom, with something regal in her carriage: do people still say "carriage"? His mother treated words as if they were coins—counted them out, was frugal. Ciro's similar with speech: he understands its value as currency, and at the same time he's spendthrift with Latin and southern charm both.

Dynamite combination.

Sometimes I think *class*. Ciro's brother Raúl's wife Luz has jet eyes and brows, full features. I can't tell if she's pretty because she's bleached her hair past brunettes' reddish color to a grayed lifeless blond and thinks it's bee-yoo-tee-fool. They live in Miami now. I bet her taste would be different if she lived somewhere else. Mine certainly would. For years every time I went home I bought pink shoes or yellow ones, colors I can't possibly wear in New York, even in summer.

Sarah once asked me to find something in her closet and I was struck by how boring it all was: grays and browns and blacks, but that's what I wear too. If I'd stayed in Florida I'd dress in bright prints, hot pinks to fight with my hair, and tangerines, lime greens, searing sun-yellows. *So*, I thought briefly, *how can you separate class from place?* But I was working on a story, so I let it go and anyway they're probably inextricable.

We didn't have money and Ciro's people, though immigrants, did. Maybe that was part of it. His father would've disapproved. And my father? Hard to know.

And my mother wasn't even in the equation in those days—pretty sorry, that is.

Ciro's immigrant family would have had to learn what we knew by birthright. It's a good thing I was born here; I could never have mastered this stuff. Though we didn't have money, we were educated and familiar with Southern ways—and American and Jewish ways.

We had a circuit-riding rabbi for a while when I was young. I ought to try to tell my children about those days—*my* days. They have no idea...

What one learns naturally in the family—I know now—is a *lot* of information—information that's obscure and subtle, and important. And hard to learn if you have to do it consciously.

So the ground Ciro's people stood on was much less stable, though they set about getting quite a lot of it, quantity making up for some of what they didn't know.

Everywhere on Earth land is wealth, and immigrants have always known that capital speaks in a local accent. Which explains Ciro's fascination with money.

Which is not the same as class.

Though I know Ciro deeply, beyond words, I'm still frequently surprised. He drank a lot of bourbon at dinner. Two doubles? Three? I had a bourbon and Coke, and he'd wrinkled his nose. I'd laughed, saying, "Just the kind of girl you can't take anywhere..." He hadn't paid attention. He has an uncanny way of knowing when to. More accurate: he knows me better than I know myself. Not better than: before.

After we've been together, I am heartened and stronger. I'm typing very slowly because these words aren't right. Something comes to me from him. A profound caring.

Its real name is love.

Love: *I love pink. Oh, I just loved that movie. I love ice cream, your house, dog, car...*We haven't the language. Or we have it, but it doesn't bear.

Between us there's a singularity, which technically is a tear in space-time where the laws of physics break down and anything is possible. Both true and impossible. His love wraps me in an airy invisible silk spun from ferocity and rapture.

Why am I writing this autobiographical thing? I put aside two new fictions to do it—about women who transgress, who violate their cultural requirements, and they're engaging, but I keep having to come back to my life, the narrative I tell myself. "We had the experience but missed the meaning," Eliot says somewhere.

One bright red bohemian cut-glass bead has more meaning when it's strung properly, next to either a family—yes, a family—of other cut-glass beads, or an ornament specially designed to bring out its particularities and sparkle. So I tell myself my life. Because it's necessary to understand it, and because it's nearly over.

Excessive.

Also true.

So I decided I would give myself this time, as if I were my own client. I'd spend an hour each workday putting it all down—to the degree that's possible—looking closely and studying.

Not because it's important or because I want my children to know it.

God forbid!

For me. Because it was. *Is,* though some day in the not-too-far-distant, it will all of it be past tense.

I read to learn the world, which is composed of people's experiences. So mine, while not more valuable than anyone else's, are part of that: we make the world, we who have lived in it.

I learned from Toss that looking hard teaches you. Looking closely is a way of knowing, and if you're writing your life you're looking. It turns out all my work is about what it's possible to know.

The next morning Rory had to leave early; he'd paid for darkroom time. Standing while he drank his coffee, he described the portfolio he's putting together, kissed me hurriedly and left. Angela would take me to the airport. We ate a nice little breakfast she made. It was the first time I'd spent any time alone with my daughter-in-law, and I liked it—girly stuff, I thought, but then she said she had something she wanted to tell me. I studied her topaz eyes, which had dark-green and yellowy glints like light on stones beneath a lake-surface. Passive-looking eyes but of course they aren't; expression's in the muscles around them.

"I told Rory I was going to tell you," she began, "And I don't know why but I want you to know. I was married before Rory."

I was stung, somehow.

Why? I had certainly never thought about whether she was a virgin. Didn't need for her to be. So what was this? I'll be dead and they'll be an old married couple one day; it's between them, has nothing to do with me. I remember thinking that.

When your daughter-in-law's talking, you are not thinking about your own sexual history.

"I was seventeen."

Half her life ago, just about.

"Ran off after the prom," she went on. "We thought it would be fun. Embarrassing, isn't it?" She's graceful. I couldn't have pulled this off with such quiet.

"No." I smiled. "Not embarrassing. I married Rory's father when I was nineteen, and he already had Rory and Bonita. My people thought I was a mess."

She laughed, clearly relieved, and poured more coffee.

"We were married six months," she said.

She has great presence.

"It was annulled," she said, "but it's not as if it didn't happen."

Huge and insignificant, present and unreal. I didn't know what to do with it. "What do you do with it?"

She looked perplexed. Naturally.

"I was thinking it's important and not important, both. Is it?"

Now she laughed. "Yes! that's it exactly. You must be a really good therapist," she said, leaning a bit in my direction.

"I hope so!"

At the airport I kissed her goodbye and thought, Well, now you're one of us.

Dearest Charles, my teacher, would've said *It's the damage.*

She'd been seventeen. The age when I first loved Ciro. The age I am when I'm with him, remarkably.

It was Charles who first suggested the writing. He knew how much becomes available as the tips of the fingers hit the keys. As if knowing resides in the body.

Which in fact, it does

"At the tip of the pen the line," Clarice Lispector, the Brazilian writer, says. And what have I learned from the writing? I believe I'm beginning to understand that the love I have given and taken, the love that has come to me unbidden, even unrecognized, is enormous, that it is the same great love that stories in literature and history are made of.

In dark and empty days, in winter, this sustains.

Some days—I don't think it often enough—I think, It's a gift from the Universe.

What I know now: all the great stories are stories of the lives of ordinary people—like us, who loved as imperfectly and as deeply as we do—for our brief time here.

I write about what I don't understand: violence, relationships, men. These are, unfortunately, not unrelated. As a consequence the daily does not appear here, but it's mostly where I spend my life, the days flying by with terrifying gathering momentum. How have I spent it between September and January? Working. Visiting with friends, dinners with friends and colleagues, long phone conversations with the children. Shopping and seeing my consultant and going to museums and movies, an ordinary life without any drama in it.

At the moment it's sleeting against my windows with a lovely *tak-tak-tak*.

The men bring the drama. *Are* the drama. Great dark blue velvet curtains rise slowly, majestically, and behind them stands (trumpet overture—ta-da):

Ciro.

I am doubled over with laughter. It's true, though. A man made of ordinary clay, as I am.

Minds are mysterious. Laughing as I write this; they'll come and get my license—I wonder what Ciro remembers. Me, clearly, as he told me that night after my father died. But what else. What does he remember about events with his wife—social events and private ones? I wonder how they're arranged in his mind, like rooms in the "memory palace," like puzzle pieces scattered, apparently random—but mind's not random—or like crystals growing, each its own structure. Tab A into Slot B. Chemical receptors: we know about those. But even heavy neurology hasn't yet explained why casual memories can have great import.

Once I saw a boy emerging from a paint store— this was maybe four years ago—a hulking young teenager probably not yet comfortable in his body, wearing a red wool cap pulled down over his ears and one of those bulky dark-blue down jackets. He held the door ajar with his body and in both arms carried two or three gallons of paint. It must've been something in the way he stood in space that took me into another place: I was overwhelmed with longing for the days when Rory was a teenager, when Michael was, and swept by the recognition of how quiet they've become, my sons.

All this was immediate: a flash of crowds of boys playing basketball or catch, shouting and groaning dramatically, the wonderful timbre of young male voices. And my sons roughhousing—sometimes with their sisters—the thudding upstairs over the kitchen. I'd stop and lift my head as if it were possible by concentrating to know what they were doing and laugh. Or I'd go to the steps and call. Sometimes I'd have to go up there and pry them apart using my own body as a lever.

Tears. I wondered if it was my youth I was grieving, or the ordinariness of children coming and going, all that tumult and natural and unextraordinary joy, reached into my bag for a Kleenex, and when I looked up the boy with the paint had gone.

At the time I thought I'd forget it, but I didn't. It remains, like my visit to Edinburgh Castle on a brilliant summer day. I saw a dog there with a face like a Hereford—very disturbing, dog with a bovine face, like some kind of corrupt cross-bred creature out of medieval tales.

And I remember standing there on the parapet trying not to look at the cannons gleaming in the sun, studying the way the light glittered on the Firth—as if it were aluminum—thinking, These people's pictures are going to have strangers in them, and I will be one of them.

I will go home with them to some little dorp in Southern Africa, or a city: maybe Toss's city, or Cape Town, Nairobi, Dar, cities I will never get to—I know that now. Or I'll appear in someone's wooden house under the *whoosh* of rainfall during the monsoon season in Penang. Why is this appealing? It's like magic, the image of your familiar self taken as in dreams to a faraway land. I love thinking I could go to Hong Kong or Tierra del Fuego or Spitsbergen— there's still time, E, I tell myself.

So it was not such a surprise to me—though it was to the children—that my short story collection was going to be called Photo Album, or Photographs from Abroad. The three stories I'd already published had surprised me, taken by the first places I'd sent them—beginner's luck, I told myself, but then an editor called to ask for others. And one day, Carlene, an agent.

It was a mild rainy mid-January day. Two clients, with flu and bronchitis, had cancelled, and I was deep in financial records so I could plan to see my tax man with everything up-to-date, when the phone rang and a woman said she was Carlene Sullivan. "I read your story 'Pandemonium' in *Solstice*," she said, "And wondered if you have other stories you want to place. I'm a literary agent."

"Good heavens," I believe I said out loud.

I met Carlene at a vegetarian bistro—what does that *mean?* I thought when she offered the description—on Third near Sixty-Eighth. Bright and blond, it had potted trees and flowers blooming here and there, and a general feeling of well-being. From giving up meat, no doubt. It was the time of year I buy gardenias. Just the week before I'd bought new plants for my office and my bedroom, their dark-green leaves glossy and the scent of flowers rich and tropical and evocative.

"Short stories are in right now, and first collections are particularly difficult," Carlene told me, "But you have a certain seriousness fused to whimsy that's appealing, that I'd like to see more of, out there."

"Out there." I can feel myself grimace. I have to move all this media-speak and pop-culture aside consciously—it's distracting.

Carlene's tawny short hair was charming and spiky, her white shirt crisp, her skirt a tiny cylinder of something that looked like leather but couldn't be, because it was a veggie place, you wouldn't wear animal skins here...

I could feel myself grinning. "That's nice," I said. "Nice to hear, nice to think." On my way back to the office, walking up Third Avenue, I heard myself say "Oh shit," This was going to complicate things with Rosa MacBride. Majorly.

Ciro told me this story: his brother Raúl was awakened one morning by a frantic hammering on his jalousied front door. I have only to hear the word *jalousies* and there's the *rattle* of little glass shelves in their metal frames. "And when he went to the door, a ragged youngster was standing there, boy about the age of Raimundo," he said, Raúl and Luz's son who had moved to California with his girlfriend and a bunch of other kids. "Raúl's unhappy. Kid's much too American."

"The immigrant tragedy," I said.

"¿?"

"Your brother comes here for a better life and his kids become people who can't be at home in the family and don't speak the language."

"Sí. Refuse to speak it."

"You don't have that with your children."

"I chose America."

"Not exactly," I said.

He nodded. "The boy at the door," he went on, "was just up from Cuba."

"'Just up.'"

When he laughed, I thought, He loves to tell stories.

Telling your life, as my clients do, is one thing—though of course, they're stories too—but telling stories for the pure pleasure in the telling, that's what he was doing. It's not, however, what I do, even though I write them. "He had taken a fiberglass boat out of Malecón to go fishing. The wind came up and he looked around at the water, the current was right, so he left." He grinned. "Amazing, no?"

"Verdad." I was thinking of wrenching change and loss. Ciro, naturally, was thinking of adventure. "How many hours does it take?" I ought to know this.

"Varies. Took him seventeen."

"Under that sun!"

"Some of it was at night."

I made a face.

"It can take three days—or forever. There's a southward current—called the Cuban Countercurrent."

"Sounds political." I couldn't resist.

He grinned.

"Can I use this?"

"Use?"

"For a story. I've published some short fiction, Ciro."

He didn't seem surprised—barely interested. A lot of times I've tried to tell Ciro who I am and what matters to me. I would not tolerate this in someone else, but it doesn't seem to matter to him. Astonishing. Or he hears it and doesn't respond because he figures I'll say what I need to. Without the grit of the daily.

Maybe he doesn't need the details because he's got the essentials. Lord.

I feel myself putting off dealing with the MacBride business.

But I've learned this: after I move the mental furniture that's standing in front of it, it'll clear the way and I'll just *do* it; it'll be effortless, because I didn't force it.

"Are you coming to Florida this winter?" Ciro asked in early December. It didn't occur to me that his fling might be over.

"Probably," I said, deciding on the spur. "I could stay with my stepmother and buy furniture for the condo."

"We don't have to tell anybody you're here," he said, which I took to be as overt an invitation as he was capable of just then.

"I'll let you know."

Even if I stayed with him I'd have to see her, my stepmother. She was old and alone and needed company.

Ciro in my life is like having a number of clocks, each set to a different decade. If my life were sci-fi, everything that happened would depend on which clock I looked at. I wish I had more imagination about time. I can only imagine it running linearly and running out. I'm in the last third, which, sometimes, I see as a white satin ribbon coiled in the moment I find myself, but as I take the next step, I see it unfurling—

So in late January, I flew home again. Told everybody I needed a few days away from the New York winter, but in fact I was going to see Ciro. It had happened, what I sensed that night he gave me the beach—not the condo: I could've bought that myself, had I thought about it. The night he gave me the beach, I knew I needed him in my life. He'd become a kind of ballast.

I love flying. Even with all the crowding and the stupid "security," I love climbing over gritty New York and watching the colors lose definition. The buildings: from a series of reddish charcoal-grays and then grays, we move up beyond the clouds, and I'm out of time. It's like being some kind of charged particle in motion in a way not possible on Earth. Every moment, I'm somewhere else. Nobody can find me, nobody can call.

They can nowadays, but I make believe it's not possible. I love this time aloft, going, not there yet.

From high above the Earth, I sometimes imagine a net thrown over the world—the actual one is longitude and latitude, and there's a myth about Indra's net, at the junctions of which, where the strands cross, there are diamonds—or in some versions pearls—and they all reflect one another. My net is something like that: at the junctures of my metaphysical net major events fly bright flags, or in some imaginings, they shine. Today I'm en route toward time with Ciro. Or I walk through the streets of a foreign city and into a lecture, and meet a man, and he turns out to be Liam. If I were far enough out I'd be able to see the trajectory, Liam walking toward the event, stunning and flamboyant. And me.

And what if such events left shining trails on the world that were invisible to the naked eye, but you could see from a thousand miles out? What bright paths we'd inscribe as we moved toward one another, neither of us knowing.

There's something absolutely glorious about the potential—not knowing.

Of course it's true of cancer, too. You could have it and be walking into the next day of your life and *zap!* No future—or none you can bear to think about—

There it is: the Skyway stretching over clear turquoise, the land's familiar curves, offshore islands like puzzle pieces, tan and sandy, set like paving stones in a pattern that can't be read from here but makes a brilliant kind of sense when seen from space.

We come in over the sandy littoral, the keys lying almost level with the flat blue Gulf, slate-blue in the lowering dark. I get off the plane into air fragrant with moisture and the familiar, into the Florida evening. There's never a thick layer of dirty ice over everything here. It's where I learned *banyan, royal poinciana.* Royal palm. Gumbo-limbo. We had a small stand of them at the back of the yard when I was a child, wonderful trees with red bark that peels off in long strands, leaving a number of different colors of red visible on the inner bark. Red and browny-mahogany, and rosy-pink; its real name is *Bursera simaruba,* which tells you its colors.

My Southern childhood—once upon a time, stripping the tough husks, I sucked thick rough stalks of sugar cane. People called me Miss Elena, which my in my father's mouth became Miscellaneous. I'm back where I was a daughter, a girl, a young woman, wife, mother. I'm back where my mother's friends were Miss Ella, Miss Hannah, Miss Louise.

I'd made reservations at my favorite hotel on Longboat Key, place I couldn't've dreamed of affording in my youth—place didn't *exist* in my youth. I took a lovely suite with peach-colored cushions and white-painted furniture, and a little glass-topped table where I could write. Hotel rooms ought to come with dictionaries and FM radios instead of Bibles and TV sets, I used to say, but now I have dictionaries on my computer. Recently someone said, of Google, Now we don't need to remember anything. Makes me wonder about the loss of cultural memory that followed the rise of print. Once upon a time people passed histories of their tribes down the generations through, poems and stories. In preliterate places, this still happens. Another thing it'd be marvelous to study But I'm here, in the *now,* so I turn on CNN, a luxury I don't indulge at home, keeping it on mute, and occasionally glancing at the flickering images—mostly wars. You can be sure there are wars somewhere every single day in the world.

Weather too. I like watching the cloudforms over Africa and China and South Korea. I like imagining Toss in Durban, that beautiful brown boy. I like imagining someone like me—and people not like, old wrinkled people with other languages and other hopes and expectations—going about the daily, all the sights and sounds and smells absolutely different from where I sit in south Florida on the Gulf, watching television.

I wonder how I've processed Liam's foreignness. When I try to think about it, it's not who he is, it's the intangibles, an emblem of which is his dark red passport lying on the dresser with his change and keys—a very different history and loyalties.

And in close, none of this pertains.

When we talk or when we touch—it's like a flavor or a tone. A substance without location.

Next morning, out by seven, I walked along the beach, the sand so cold it hurt. My feet were going numb, but how could I leave? The water was blue and featureless. There must be an infinite range of blues. I've seen it aquamarine, pale and silvery like a mirror. Emerald, navy. I've seen it turquoise all the way down to sand. Sometimes it stripes over a sandbar, blue and yellow and light green, but today it was flat all the way to Texas, where my Caroline's teaching art at a small private college outside Galveston. She couldn't believe it was the same Gulf: "It's terrible here, Mother, full of white stuff like soapsuds on the waves, and oil and crud..." Crud, word I hadn't known was still in circulation.

I went in for breakfast finally, my legs aching with the cold, though the rest of me felt terrific.

More terror in the newspapers, more murder. I should've brought a book to the table. While I dawdled over my toast and coffee, a waiter asked if I were Dr. Summerfield. Oh no, I thought, who's tracked me here?

I expected him to bring a phone, but he came back with a vase of pale pink roses and a card that said *C.*

Nice touch.

Then I drove all the way out to the end of Longboat on Gulf of Mexico Drive, the old road that runs the length of the Key and used to end in a sandy track where now it's connected to Anna Maria by a bridge. Progress.

Heading back toward town, I looked for places we used to go skin-swimming. High-rise hotels obscure the water on Gulf and Bay sides, both. Absolutely familiar and utterly strange. I drive everywhere by feel and never get lost, and every visit reminds me what-all's gone, my mother and father. Most of my life.

Of the Florida I knew, just about every trace has been erased—or superseded. But I know its nature, and beneath the surface faint images remain of what was here when I was young, and when all this is gone, what'll be here still.

Until the Gulf rises, and it all goes under.

I listened to radio stations with the same call-letters I'd grown up with: WSPB, and from Tampa, WFLA. Almost expected the same old music—what I got was disco, some gospel, pop stuff, which, since the children have moved out, I no longer know.

Weather-guy said it was 69° with 80% humidity. "We're ninety-seven percent accurate over the last one hundred forecasts." Rory would've said "Well wow." He used to coach Michael: "Say it without expression."

What a weird lesson, I'd say, to which one of them would reply, flat "That's why we call it deadpan, ma'am."

What it was, I see now, was the older brother teaching the younger male ways.

After my tour of Longboat I drove out through town to Siesta Key, passing my old high school—now a *museum.* I believe I shrieked.

Maybe my favorite place in the world, Siesta still has some old houses drowning in miles of ropy lianas or hidden away under canopies of banana and traveler's palms; sandy yards with stands of pine and eucalyptus. Gray fronds of Bismarck palms. Everything you need grows here: plumy grasses, sea grape, six-foot schefflera and bright-speckled croton. Cactus, agave, citrus bearing golden fruit like trees full of suns. Gardenia, lemon, mango, guava. I looked for the gumbo-limbo, which I've seen in Pelican Cove and at Selby Gardens, but didn't find any on the Key. Maybe I'll buy one for the condo Ciro gave me; I hadn't thought, I get to do a yard here!

I stopped at a little market to get postcards to send the children. "Are there still two high schools here?" I asked the girl at the checkout.

She looked surprised. "Booker T. Washington's an arts high school," she said, brushing easily past what had to have been years of pain and fraught negotiation.

Drove up and down streets between Osprey and the Trail where friends used to live, remembering Maureen's slumber parties, getting drunk with Gloria and Liz. Trying hash. Where is Betty Jane? We walked everywhere in those days. Once I wore a striped dress—a loud aqua-blue color I've never worn since— in a rainstorm; I was walking up South Pineapple toward Main Street in this dress, which had high-heeled shoes to match, though I don't remember the occasion for such dressing-up. To save the shoes from steamy rain coursing over the streets and swirling along gutters, I had taken them off and was walking barefoot through downtown, my shoes in my hand. One of my friends was with me, but for the life of me I can't remember who.

All these memories. I love knowing it's possible to evoke most of them with electrical stimulation. The colors and textures and scents I experienced have become part of the wiring. My history, enfleshed.

On the way back to Longboat, I stopped at St. Armand's Key, which once was *the* place to shop, and had to take myself to lunch at Columbia. The best Spanish food in town used to be at The Palm, but it's been out of business a long time, and now all that was left was this very good Cuban restaurant whose home base is Tampa. I had a delicious lunch of black bean soup and chorizos, mild and sweet, and wonderful Cuban bread slathered with butter. My kosher grandparents would turn over in their graves.

I called Ciro, who over time had given me about seventeen numbers. "If you need me I'll be at…" I'd dutifully written them all down and think I kept them, but some are probably no longer in use. I'd starred the cell, home, and office phones, but I wasn't sure which was which, and left messages on two.

He called at six and said he was tied up. Tomorrow? How long would I be there? Why wasn't I using the condo?

"I haven't furnished it yet."

"Go see Marty Gaspari, he's got a lot of nice stuff."

I didn't want to go see Marty Gaspari.

"Here's his number."

I even wrote it down.

"Tomorrow?"

"What time?" Now I was annoyed, thinking, it's a bit late for me to hang around waiting for a man. Even this one.

"I'll call you," he said.

"I'll be out."

"Cell?"

I didn't speak.

"I'll leave word. Sweetheart."

"I'd like to know: lunch or dinner?"

"Dinner."

"Fine. See you."

Darlin', sweetheart. Señor Suave. Mierda.

I spent the next day with my stepmother. Lord, spare us. She's old, she's in pain, she's desolate. Even if you've had a busy intellectual life, which I have, when your vision and hearing go…What a crummy design, that we have to go toward this, knowing.

Again and again she says *It's hard to get old.* Even repetition doesn't convey the terrible diminishing.

I took her shopping. The salesgirl was about twelve. Twenty. She was rude to Anna-Louise, and I went to the manager. "Oh, don't fuss," Anna-Louise said, "She'll get old some day." Yeah, I thought, but we won't be around to enjoy it.

And in fact it echoed something clients've talked about, and I've been getting intimations of: old women do not exist.

There are lots of theories about this: old people are not attractive (but in Africa and Asia "attractive" is irrelevant). I think their—*our*—presence repudiates the culture of youth here, where everybody's stuck at puberty. Check out any sitcom, most movies.

She tottered. I held her elbow. I took her to lunch. "Where would you like to go?" Perhaps the fact that her horizons are now so limited helps in the letting go, but when she said "Friendly's," I wanted to weep.

In an attempt to focus poor eyes, she stared and I watched people's annoyance or discomfort: they thought she was finding fault. She could barely see them.

We mostly reminisced about my father, which was hard for me, but clearly what she needed.

I took her home and settled her in, promising to come again. "Are you seeing Ciro?" she said.

"Tonight for dinner."

"He's always been crazy about you, darlin'."

"He sure doesn't show it," I said. But I hadn't told her about the condo.

As I drove back to Longboat I realized she wasn't talking all the time anymore. Poor thing, she was running out of energy—which may be one definition of dying, a gradual loss of energy.

Lord, please give me the strength to kill myself before things get to this.

My favorite death-fantasy is, I'm striding up (or down) Madison Avenue on a sunny bright May day in buffeting winds and drop dead.

When Ciro came at seven I was waiting. It was the first time I'd seen him since Boston, and I wasn't sure what was going to happen.

It's clear now that he called all the shots. Every one of them.

Michael once said I was in what he called "the hinge" generation—between unquestioned male dominance everywhere, he meant, and the first wave of feminism. And I was determined by my family and the local culture: it was Florida, where girls were brought up with very different expectations than my daughters in New York.

Ciro took me to a restaurant clear on the other side of town, almost to Venice, where we wouldn't be going this time. All the way, he talked, about his children, the sort of yield he was getting in the groves; prices. And of course stocks and bonds and taxes. I listened in a way I didn't realize I had learned to, with a kind of soft-focus. Occasionally I asked a question. Mostly the sound of his voice washed over me like warm rain.

As we walked from the parking lot into the restaurant, his arm around my shoulders, he hummed "Guantanamera."

"What're you thinking?"

He was remembering family gatherings, he said, how his cousins, and Raúl and he, and their wives— he looked a bit abashed as he said *wives*—would sing it. "Did you know that Martí wrote the words?"

"So it's political."

"Sí. Covertly. It's one of those songs people improvise to, has countless versions."

"I didn't know that."

I saw them gathered in a finca—not an actual house on real land here in Florida, but an imagined place—a coastal Cuban place open to the sea—humid winds coming in over the blue water and the golden littoral, singing, firelight playing over their faces. Firelight like shadows leaping from smudge pots on winter nights: I'd grown up with those. Flames and shadows on the dark.

I saw their faces, his father and mother, Raúl and Luz, he and Liz, his first wife—and imagined their names in his parents' mouths: *loose* and *lease*. What was his second wife's name? I couldn't retrieve it. Sarabeth? Sara-Louise? Some double name. Sara-Anne?

Marylou! Lord, my file-system's going to hell. Neither of his wives was Cuban. Why had I never thought of this? His wives were part of his attempt reconcile his personal and social strangeness with this place—where he had grown up, son of immigrants. His wives were Anglo: they belonged.

Typical American story.

Sometimes my mind runs off like a puppy escaping the leash. I thought: It's a good thing he's not going to marry me. If his father were alive a third American wife would be certain proof Ciro had no judgment at all.

The restaurant was quiet, expensive, and the servers obsequious, their presence a wall of flesh. Ciro liked it. "They're supposed to make things comfortable."

"Can you tell them to back away?"

He laughed and didn't, so I had to ignore them.

I'm a repository for countless secrets. In a sense, that's my business. People tell me things and they know I won't tell anybody else. I hadn't planned, when I landed in Sarasota, to tell Ciro about what happened between Liam and me, but I did tell him. Over the three-hour dinner.

It'd been worrying at me, having been used by those people who called. Sometimes as I fall asleep I see black-and-white photos, as if Liam and I had been photographed: zoom lens, grainy film, harsh contrast. Maybe even taped.

Bedroom sounds. Jesus.

I told him about the telephone call: "We know you know Liam," and how it had played out over the course of the day. I told him I felt soiled by it.

"But not by him," he said.

"Oh, not by him! Of course not. He was soiled as well. Also. I mean…" I chose him, I thought. Maybe even said it…I can't be sure.

After a long pause he said, "He's married," with stunning quiet.

I couldn't read his eyes.

"Ciro."

"Oh my lady." *What* was he thinking? How could I be so transparent and he so opaque?

I'd called Liam opaque.

Men are fascinating because you're never going to understand them. Or: as soon as you think you've figured someone out, pow! he says *He's married.*

Then he delivered the second strike: "He's Minister for External Affairs in…"

Had I thought he didn't read the papers?

He cut into his steak. "Sí," he said, "So you play now with the beeeg boys," in a Cuban accent, soft "s" on "boys."

I understood right then: he wanted to be my most important man. Without intending, I'd underscored what he saw as his subordinate   position. I flooded with sorrow to've caused such . . . humiliation.

Or it didn't have everything to do with me, I thought, considering that competitive male thing. So it shouldn't have surprised me that next he began to talk about schemes and shifting alliances among sugar growers, about state government and change, politics in the Citrus Commission.

"Things've been very tough. We had that stunning freeze in '82, and then the canker. I lost sixty-six thousand acres with the canker alone."

"I remember reading about that."

"Did you?"

"I tend to follow the news about citrus. They burned the trees."

"Had to."

"I thought it was like killing something alive."

"It was," he said, matter-of-fact. "Not as bad as BSE."

Nothing registered.

"Mad cow," he said.

"Oh. Yes. No, not that bad. But I remember feeling terrible about it. It was around that time that farmers spilled milk onto the ground to keep prices up. D'you remember that?"

A faint affirmation.

"I was real upset about that," I said. "Poor children in cities—not just our cities: all over the world—and they spilled hundreds of thousands of gallons of milk."

"I don't like to see food wasted."

I saw the groves burning. "Where?"

"Some here in Sarasota County, some over to Alturas."

"Which is…?"

"Southeast of Bartow."

I consulted the map in my head. "North."

He nodded, and told me what I'd known, a bit. "My father had a strip along the Ridge"—a feature of the land that runs north-south like a spine in Central Florida, he meant—"Up near Bartow almost to Avon Park. It wasn't contiguous, but it was a lot of acreage. To get me started, he gave me several thousand acres. Said, 'You'll grow sugar,' which he'd done in Cuba. But a lot of it was too far north for sugar, and citrus, even with the losses, is an easier crop to market. Do you know," he said, "Some years ninety percent of the orange crop goes into concentrate."

"Smell of Dade City," I grimaced.

"After all that trouble in the groves I invested in livestock, bought seventeen hundred head of cattle, and decided to run for office. In Miami."

"How'd you choose Miami?"

He smiled. "I have a home there."

"Total houses?"

"Right now? Three."

"Oh, that's not so many…"

He laughed. "At one time I did have four."

"Someday, when I have twenty years, I'm going to try to figure out what I was doing while you were bopping from one home to another…office to grove to ranch—"to woman.

He laughed.

You've claimed all of Florida, I thought.

"It's like dual citizenship," he was saying. Holding office in Miami, I keep faith with my fathers Though he wasn't talking about his own father, I wondered again how old his father was when he'd died for La Lucha. Probably, he'd been about our age now—late fifties, early sixties.

Time closed like a Chinese screen, all those little figures painted by hand, details with a one-hair brush—what labor. Ciro watched me.

"I can't imagine loyalty to a country."

"You don't have to."

"That's right."

"Sí. It's a particularly twentieth-century problem, though not uniquely." He does this: every once in a while his speech is so precise it takes me by surprise. He doesn't take language for granted as I do. Because it's my native tongue. Because I revise all the time?

Then he shrugged and sipped his drink. "I can't go home, but I can participate in the home my countrymen have made here." This was probably the most emotional thing he'd ever said. "Talk was, I'd come down there to take advantage of the Cuban vote, but I've owned property in Miami for thirty years. I sent my children to school there. I'm an American Cuban. Why should I not take advantage of the Cuban vote?"

"Did you ever see this?" He finished a mouthful of salad and wiped his mouth. Then, reaching for his wallet, he dug out a picture photocopied from *The*

New Yorker, and again I was jolted: did I think he read nothing? "La Isla," it said at the top, over a sea of words which at first glance looked like lines of random letters, the shape of Cuba cut out of it. "Cuba as negative space," I said. A thud in my chest.

He nodded.

"Or if laid on top, positive." I lifted it closer to read the little black marks: *marmarmarmarmarmar,* row after row.

"It seems to say *armas,*" I said, "But it doesn't; it says *mar, mar, mar.*"

"Sí. Your eye makes other words from the letters."

Mama, I saw too.

"Who's the artist?"

"Writer. Guillermo Cabrera Infante."

"Amazing," I said, registering *Guillermo.* "Terrific. Looks like *warn,* too, even though that's not there—the letters conjure it."

"My father wanted to fly in and not come out until we had Castro's head on a pike. Now I think how located in a specific time that idea was," he said.

I waited.

"Things change," he shrugged.

But *things* are what we've built our lives on, I thought, The specific realities and expectations of our times. In some sense we expect permanence. Regardless...of what we know.

"Ferociously anti-Communist period," he said. "HUAC. You know."

"I do know, but here's something amazing, Ciro: I learned all of it after I left here. My people didn't talk politics." McCarthy might never have happened, I was thinking, when he laughed. "I used to wish mine didn't. My father spent a lot of money on those crazy missions—and some not so crazy. He helped bring a lot of people over…"

"I know," I said. "My father used to tell me about your father's…" *exploits* was the only word I could come up with … Missions?"

He nodded. Then he said, "It's hard to know what anybody believes."

Including yourself, I thought. "¿Su madre?"

"You can *tu* me," he said.

I felt slapped. "I should know that," I said.

"Claro. As for my mother," he shrugged, "No sé."

I nodded, wondering if he'd ever asked her.

"How is she?"

"She's in a terrible place," he said, looking off. "She's very sharp, but there are so many things wrong—she's having a bad time. Seems somebody shouldn't have a bad time at the end, it's not like she's going to learn anything from it."

I'd thought that. When William died. When Rachel. "I know," I said, finally, thinking of the old colonial buildings along the waterfront in Havana, crumbling, going back to sand. "I'm so sorry."

"Me too. She seems not to've gotten over Abby's death. I was in New Guinea when she died. Nobody could reach me…" his eyes watered. His daughter had been twenty-one, first child, only daughter. His *child*.

"I can't imagine," I said.

Phoebe's youthful image floated into the silence. She'd be close to sixty. Who could comprehend this? Time collapsed, slackened, and pulled taut—by whose hand?—and without volition, you were sprung from its insubstantial surface. *Sprung*. I'll say. My eyes burned.

He didn't say anything else about Liam. *Southern gentleman* has many meanings. In college, when a boy came for a date the dorm desk would buzz our rooms—this was in the dark ages before same-sex dorms—and say, "You have a gentleman caller."

Code for sexual promise.

Ciro offered me coffee, another drink, dessert. No, no, and no. Thank you.

We drove back to Longboat. Now I was certain I'd sleep alone that night. What did I think was going on? What did I feel? I don't remember, because when we got there he turned off the key and leaned toward me and I was a teenager again, moistening. He kissed me, hard. "Well, darlin', are you going to invite me in?"

"Only if you'll say yes," I said, tracing his beautiful lips with my fingertip.

"I'd love to," he said, "Sweetheart." He tangled his hands in my hair and said, "You have fierce hair." I heard *fire* in the word and laughed.

Where had that radical self-consciousness, and shame, gone? As I put my glasses on the night-stand I thought, It wandered off while I was busy elsewhere.

I rested my head on his chest crossed with scars and he tousled my hair. It was entirely comfortable, as if we'd been doing it since we were very young——, which in a sense we had.

I could hear his heart beating——images moved through me, knives, machines. The quiet thudding, in which I heard *shush shush shush.*

Sounds of his life in the bones of my face.

For the first time in a long life I wondered what kind of person can cut into the living flesh.

It was a distant intellectual question with no feeling attached. But I knew by now: this means it matters more than I can bear.

My mind filled with machines like the ventilator that had kept my father breathing, dull aluminum-colored box out of which poured corrugated tubes like vacuum cleaner hoses. These kept the little fist-sized muscle red and alive. The gray matter.

I held him, realizing in our quiet that I'd told him about Liam partly because I wanted him to know he wasn't the only one who had other partners.

Then I said, "Do you like this?"

Because I didn't know.

We were in our fifties, and I asked, like a schoolgirl, but not like a girl, because the question acknowledged a history.

Morning. Water-light played on the walls, wavering and rocking, panels and lozenges of light, each a different density. Reflections not only of water but of us, Ciro and me, shining and made light.

Reluctantly—Get it straight, girl: nothing lasts forever. I got up and showered and dressed. Sometimes I look at myself in the mirror in yet another gray, green, or black dress and think, Aren't you bored out of your mind? I am, but it takes too much energy to think about clothes. Every few years, frustrated and tired of it all, I buy something outrageous: orange, red, fuchsia. Yellow works, but it's got to be the right yellow. I don't find it often.

What I do still wish—and this is absurd, a woman my age—is that my eyes were a beautiful clear ice-green. Or blue, like sky; but no, they're a dark boring green, unmistakably green, but not interesting. With gold and brown flecks, which of course I never see anymore.

Over breakfast, thinking about how different our dreams were, and how well-matched our bodies, I was going to tell him a story that would say a bit about who I am and what matters to me, and as I talked, I realized: all this time I've thought he hasn't been hearing me, but fact is, E, you have not been hearing him.

The man's smitten.

Something shifted in my breast, and then a wave of grief: my *su* at dinner.

I drew a deep breath, but it was ragged. I felt his gaze on me.

I drank my tea, attending to the scrambled eggs.

"My lady," he said, soft.

I nodded, my eyes full of water, but I couldn't look up. "Excuse me." I went to the restroom.

When I came back, I told him the story. "Once, when I was living in Rye with Terry, we were visited by the Christmas Committee."

He laughed.

He had ordered steak and eggs, as if he were still an athlete, not the sort of thing a man nearly sixty who's had two heart operations should have for breakfast. I don't know why I was amused.

"I open the door and—picture this, Ciro—there was my neighbor. I'm at the door, and behind me the children are squabbling over dinner. Six children make a great deal of noise. She had a suit on, and a puppy in her arms which," I drawled, "was wearing a little red sweater. You're a man, you've probably never had this experience: I answer the door and the kids are making all kinds of anti-social racket and I look like hell, no makeup, I'm wearing jeans and a sweatshirt or something, and bare feet, 'cause I never wear shoes—a legacy of my South…" I broke off to laugh at him. He wears expensive loafers, probably leaves them right outside the shower-door, which in my history and imagination is sandblasted with cattails and flamingoes. Sarah used to call them *Plamíngoes,* and Rory *Flaming Oh's.*

She was so sorry to bring this up, but had I noticed how lovely the street looked? I said yes, it surely did look fine, and—genteel as pie, she huffed and puffed. I ignored it. Would she like to come in and have a cup of tea, we were just finishing dinner…? If she'd said yes, I'd have died, 'cause of the mess. She appreciated it, but, and wanted to know if I'd noticed that the street looked almost perfect, and would probably win the Jaycees' contest for the prettiest Christmas-tree-lights-street, or the Most Welcoming Decorations— but it was looking just a bit drab right about here and when were we planning to put up our decorations, because the judges would be around in two more days.

'Well, I said, I'm really sorry but I don't think we can participate.

"And why would that be?" she asked, a bit testy by now.

I should've replied in the subjunctive: that might be because we're Jewish. Instead I said, "Well, we're Jewish, and so we don't have Christmas decorations."

Ciro had put down his steak-knife and fork and was looking at me with what in someone less socially-aware and experienced would've passed for disbelief.

"We'd really like to help, but…But they were trying to make us feel guilty, Terry said later. At the time I didn't catch the guilt. I felt sorry for her, this stupid street seemed to matter so much."

"Not sorry enough," Ciro said, a smile playing around his eyes.

"Not quite. Then Terry came to the door and administered the coup de grace, said maybe he would put something in the window over his side of the bed, which at the time I thought was funny but now seems unnecessarily unkind " And unlike Terry, I thought, for the first time.

"I've noticed," Ciro nodded, "Cruelty becomes less fun as we mature."

"Excellent. D'you suppose we have to learn to be kind?"

"Seems so."

"You have the prettiest mouth I have ever in my life seen on a man," I said, surprised when the color rose in his face.

"We belonged to a synagogue then," I told him, "And some of the people there were purely offended, said it was insulting, her coming by like that, but I figured they just didn't know any Jews."

"In New *York*?" said Ciro.

"Right," I said. "Caught."

"Caught with respect to…?"

"Some kind of ridiculous innocence, naiveté. ¿Cómo se dice en Español?"

"Ingenua. Inocente."

That didn't seem to mean what I intended. How could I tell him I'd never really belonged to the synagogue, though we paid astronomical dues? That

I'd been unable to find myself there. Sometimes I thought it was all those New Yawwwk accents, but I knew. It was having been a Jew in South Florida in those days. Rural South Florida, if you please, ma'am. I must've talked about it in analysis for forty hours, not belonging.

I tried to tell him.

"Like me," he said.

Back in New York, they were side by side in my mind, Liam and Ciro. Ciro's dual citizenship. In Liam's mouth, "dual" became "jewel." *Jewel carriageway.* Duty was *djuti,* which sounded so like *Jew-ty* the first time I heard it, I'd had to stop and replay it, as if on slow.

I would send him an amaryllis, Ciro. Without a real winter, you don't need one, so probably he'd never seen one. They come from Toss's country—they ought to grow at home.

San Francisco

Now that I had an agent and some stories were beginning to appear, I'd have to talk with my clients. They'd never believe me. Never.

A sweep of despair. How would I deal with this? Some time back, I'd told Trish, a colleague at the Institute, that I'd been in Liam's country and had begun a group of stories set there. I could not believe it when she said, "Oh, people told you stories and you wrote them down?"

"I *made them up.*" I said, my voice metal on stone.

I've thought about this a lot by now. They're a gift from the subconscious. From careful watching, William would've said. "The novelist is necessarily a moral psychologist," he told me once. And the short story writer? I wish William were here so I could tell him: short stories suit my temperament; a fifty-minute enterprise—though it takes many times fifty minutes to make them seem so.

They come from letting myself think a whole range of things.

It's not possible to say it accurately—even to myself. If I wrote music, people would never think they understood how it happened, but because everybody uses words—and because everybody's going to write a book one day, they just have to sit down and do it—

they think they know how it happens. Regardless of education, unless they do it they haven't a clue.

But my more immediate problem is Rosa MacBride. She will see it as competition, and I've already got enough problems dealing with her.

I wrote it all up like a loose case study to try to get hold of it:

Rosa MacBride, a forty-five-year-old successful novelist and well-known literary figure, is the author of five well-received novels, of which I have read three. They're insightful and smart and witty and interesting throughout. The author is well-connected in the New York literary world.

Two years ago when she came to see me MacBride's presenting problem was her relationship with her partner, Craig Bannister. She is also in a permanently stressful relation with her daughter Melissa, now twenty-four. Highly competitive, she raised the daughter without, in my view, adequate boundaries, treating Melissa as a friend and confidante.

To further confuse the daughter, she (mis)used her pridefully, taking all Melissa's accomplishments as consequent on her own parenting. In fact she is a careless parent, uninvolved except in the most superficial ways, and in my judgment Melissa suffers from significant emotional neglect.

MacBride has not been able to hear any of my attempts to suggest ways she might think about doing things differently with Melissa, whom she uses as a mirror in which she sees herself magnified.

As Melissa has matured, the mother has reacted to her increasing needs for autonomy—which are fused, naturally, to needs for the emotionally absent mother—by criticizing and restricting her, behaviors designed, I pointed out, to force Melissa to move out of the house, a long-overdue event which will totally devastate the mother.

Every session begins with some *situation*, as MacBride calls it, with her daughter. One time, about a month into our work together I said, And Craig. Where does he fit in with all this? and MacBride bristled: I have to talk about Melissa!

Am really up a tree here.

Up against history, too.

And the MacBride thing's complicated by my own history with my early unforgettable client Abigail. With whom I became the Bad Mother, mirroring Abigail's own behavior. Awful. Sometimes still I dream fragments of Bad Mother dreams. I'm back in training, where, of course, I'm seeing a lot of sick people and get upset, troubled, disturbed, made slightly ill, by many of them, especially the pedophiles and the really back-ward people. But the case I messed up is—naturally—the one that haunts me.

Abigail was a young white woman who came through the clinic and was referred to me on the rotation among advanced grad students (large in my mistakes was my having taken on some of the mother-role with her). Abigail had one black grandparent—her father's father. This was a source of both pride and difficulty for her, and I'm still not sure what it meant to her to be what we're now calling biracial, or multiethnic. Consequently she felt herself to be without a clear socially constructed identity.

She told her background with a kind of strong defiant thrust which I admired and took for health. I liked her, which might've been part of the problem.

Abigail was tall and heavy in a fluid very female way, big-boned and full-breasted, and probably reminded me of Rachel, but unlike my cousin, she had long straight brown hair, high cheekbones, and a graceful gait; she'd been a dancer in high school and said she would've gone on dancing had she not gotten involved with Sam, her first husband. She took an office job to help support them. Her parents had been involved with her to what seemed like a reasonable degree, and when I met her, she was in crisis over her marriage, which was eleven years old; she was twenty-nine.

As events evolved, she chose to leave her children, two and six, with their father, to make a new life in a new part of the country with a new man, and I was appalled. It was a case of over-identification, and into the mix, transference and counter-transference, a sprinkle of projection—just bucketloads of difficult, really crummy stuff. I called it evil, in those days, desperate with error and shame. Obviously this stuff is not inherently evil but sure can fuck up a therapy, which I did.

And therapy's a sacred trust. I am experienced now, and still I feel this, though I've a much more flexible attitude about whom I'm seeing.

It occurs to me too that in some way she resembled—perhaps stood in for—Gaynell, who's pretty sure she also had a black grandparent, and who is my dear friend, peer, not a client; so, in addition to everything else, there was that. Which has to do with judging her—or anger at her, or envy?—in ways I haven't even *yet* got hold of.

I hate the way this old unresolved stuff floats up to the surface and muddies it.

Which is saying I hate what's perfectly natural.

What it taught me is clear: there are issues, like leaving one's children, that I am not going to be able to deal with well.

At the beginning with a client, because presenting problems are often not apparent or fully recognized I have no idea what I'm going to be confronted with. So I sometimes find myself in a jam, and have to either figure out a way to deal with it or refer a person with whom I've already established a pretty solid connection.

I had supervision and consultation but I didn't see the traps and so I didn't bring salient issues to my supervisor or consultant. This is one of the ways I learned about my capacity for denial: lots of things I thought not pertinent were. Or: I didn't bring my irritation and annoyance, which would've signaled something.

The volume of mistakes here is—to be honest—at the edge of competence. Terrible.

Gaynell and Dan said—then and later—that both supervisor and consultant should have asked questions, should have picked up something, but they could only deal with what I brought them; it doesn't seem right to blame them for something that was clearly my responsibility.

What's left, besides the very occasional nightmares and some half-waking gray images that evoke the tone of that failure, is my realization that there are some things I cannot tolerate and am not going to be able to forgive.

This grieves me because forgiveness is necessary, humans being flawed mortal creatures who will do awful things.

I am unhappy and a bit frightened to find myself at this stage of my life really quite unforgiving.

By the time I saw what was happening with Rosa MacBride it was too late to save the therapy. Colleagues and supervisors said the obvious: her behavior acted out my repressed fears. They said I was afraid I would leave my own children. I wanted to, surely; I'd been overwhelmed so much of the time. But it wasn't repressed, and that time had passed. While I had fantasized sleep, whole weekends of it, I never wished to leave them. On the least rational levels, where we of course live, there were other connections: theory says I was furious at Phoebe for dying and leaving me her children, and at Rachel, who left Flora. And that I identified with the bereft children.

And I had to take care of them.

I can say it, but it doesn't feel true. Whatever it was, it's something I've not yet got hold of, and—it's late in the game, now, E—may never. And as for being angry because you've been left when someone dies, I know pop culture's full of this assertion but it has never felt true to me. Grief is different from anger, and—dare I say it?—in the irremediable face of death, purer.

I did identify with the daughters who'd been left behind. And was occasionally terrified—I was the mother—that something would happen to me, and then who would raise my children? I was both mother and daughter, bereaved and bereft. Violence and disease had given me two daughters and a son.

An entire family was given me.

And I didn't deserve it.

Lord.

Lord, I am not worthy.

How could they leave me—a *girl,* terrified—their *children,* those most unrelinquishable of responsibilities?

I was inadequate, so I punished Abigail, was critical and fault-finding, took a superior position that was entirely foreign to me and destructive to both of us and eroded my developing confidence in myself in my profession.

The loss of confidence hasn't gone away, which William would've said is just as well, but I'm getting tired of all this second-guessing. I don't know that it's useful anymore. One thing I know for sure: clients are strong and have many defenses and though we like to think we're so important in their lives—the awful God-complex, for which there are many, but perhaps not enough, compensatory devices—we aren't. They'll do fine without us. Mostly have done. And we're not in such great shape ourselves, many of us.

During the work with Abigail I was not unlike the way Rosa MacBride is with her daughter, so I've been really careful, talking to Luanne, my consultant, and generally being 99% non-directive. But now this new element with MacBride throws the whole operation into *spin*.

I could make such a bad mistake.

It's about forgiveness too.

Here it is:

Rosa MacBride is the judge of an important national novel competition. Each of five preliminary judges sends her five books. "Which," she told me drily, "Is one hell of a lot of books."

She came in this morning wearing an old black sweater and jeans and boots, her hair in a scarf, and no makeup. Barely controlled agitation; uncharacteristic fidgeting, twisting her many chunky silver rings. Hardly the glamorous novelist, though on the jackets of her books she's positively gorgeous.

"What's happening?"

Said she had a confession to make. Big Trouble, thought I, and after all this time. Sure enough, she's read five of the books—she's going through them systematically, one from each preliminary judge first, then the second from each…and the fifth book is by her oldest friend, Josie Ruehl-Barnett. They've been like sisters. Ruehl-Barnett has published short fiction and essays, but never a novel. Rosa didn't even know she was working on a novel. So she feels betrayed. As if she's been tricked in some way, so she's put out, angry, and jealous to the skies. This wouldn't be but a transitory problem, except that she plans to fix it so her friend's book never sees print.

Why?

She doesn't want it to.

My teeth ache.

I'm hardly the one to pontificate. Furthermore, I'm already warned. Look at the way she treats Melissa and Craig. Perhaps everybody.

But here, never. Which probably has to do with power and authority: where she has it she abuses it, and here she hasn't any. That she knows of.

Furthermore, despite her perhaps unconscious wishes that I do so, I will not tell her what to do.

So the question is, when your client does something hateful, even if you understand some of the reasons for it, what if you sit in judgment and are angry?

I'd love to tell her I'm cutting back. Or that I don't think it's working.

I can't permit myself to chicken out this way, regardless of how appealing a prospect it is. She would say, But I've played by the rules. She has. It's about me.

It's also about the ways she treats women—Melissa and now her friend "like a sister to me." God spare us sisters like this.

Four hours later, the connection's come clear:

I will reframe MacBride's treatment of her friend in terms of power, telling her some of what I've sketched here, that she comes here because the power she has in the world feels unearned...Whew.

Praise be!

The process always tells you what to do—I will document this carefully and hold onto it for a few days. Then talk with Luanne. Maybe I'll write Charles, who taught me so much of this. Bless your heart, Charles. Maybe I'll buy him a good Glenn Gould CD and send it—it's impossible to say it properly, *years* of thanks.

End of April. Liam calls, his voice a gust of sea air: "I'm visiting your country next month. Will you by any chance be in San Francisco?"

As if my country's as small as his. "I could arrange it."

"Conference. I won't have a lot of time."

"San Francisco's a great town—have you been there?"

"I have done." I can see him nodding, "Several times."

"Well, then you know how many things there are to do. I'd love to."

He gave me a Bay Area phone number. "Leave word where I can find you. I'll be there May 3-7. Oh, and prior to that, you can reach me at…"

I hate to miss New York in early May—best time of year, absolutely. Well, but Liam. I called a charming little European hotel in Union Square, one of those expensive places with pretty furnishings and a sofa— "Stay at a Motel 6," Sarah's always saying. She and Caroline both: how can they be my daughters, chorusing, What a waste of money, and You're only going to sleep there.

No, my darling daughters. Not a Motel 6. As a matter of fact I'm going to entertain an eminent statesman. Whew. Wherever Liam is, the men with the cameras can't be far off.

I'll wear sunglasses, I thought, and could not stop laughing.

How nice to just up and go. Not long ago—most of my life—I couldn't have afforded to. This year, Florida with Ciro and San Francisco with Liam: what riches! I'd been wanting to see the no-longer new modern art museum. I'd walk around Golden Gate Park. Whether things went well with Liam or not, I'd have these few days. You get off a plane in San Francisco, and for a moment, it's not possible to tell whether those purple shapes at the horizon are low cloud or hills. My first visit I actually thought: *movie backdrop.*

Who gets which numbers? I wondered, getting ready to call one of them he'd given me. There must be codes for various degrees of intimacy or security. I'd be in the outer circle.

You'd have to have a certain kind of mind to keep this sort of thing straight.

I called. Consulate? Embassy'd have to be in D.C. I know absolutely nothing. "May I speak to the secretary to the Minister for External Affairs?"

"I'll connect you." American accent. Of course they'd employ locals.

"Minister's Office." Foreign accent.

"Mr. Stephenson asked that I leave word where he could reach me, Dr. Elena Summerfield. I'll be staying at..."

It was easy, though strange, for a poor girl from South Florida. Playing with "the beeeg boys." My chest felt heavy.

He strode into the lobby at seven-thirty, where I was waiting because he was late. What a beautiful man! Large and florid, he fills his suits, which are usually wrinkled, and radiates energy and goodwill. It's in his high color and easy smile.

He kissed me briefly and put his arm around me. "Let's go, shall we? We'll get a drink there," he said, gesturing. He steered me across the street and around the corner and into a bar.

"It's not The Crown," I said, as we settled into our booth.

"Doesn't suit you?"

"Oh, it's fine." I gestured to the empty spaces around us. "I like it when it's not crowded. D'you suppose your men with the cameras are around?"

He laughed. "Doubt it."

Keep still, I told myself. Of course, he wasn't going to tell me about that phone call.

We talked about our children and work. World events were apparently off-limits. There'd been another bomb at a European airport—nobody hurt— but I didn't want to tread where I shouldn't, so I didn't tell him about the bomb at Heathrow. Suddenly, with that wonderful British efficiency—the wonderful efficiency with which they partitioned India and large chunks of Africa, Michael pointed out when I told him—a very small contingent of police drew down some gates and put a metal folding screen around a suitcase. Smooth as pie, we were moved away, another gate dropped like a portcullis, and *poof!* it was over, for us.

It would've been embarrassing to tell him about the time I took the signs seriously. This was at Stansted. **Please report any unattended luggage.** I was flying into Belfast, and at the coffee bar, I'd sat watching a lipstick-red suitcase for about forty minutes before I finally went to the British Midlands counter and said "There's a suitcase over there that's been left a really long time..."

"Probably gone to the loo," she said.

Of course all this was before September 11th.

Before our terror. Which even now, brings involuntary tears—all I need is to see an image of one of the buildings smoldering—

In those days I thought if I were planting a bomb that's just what I would do: something completely frivolous, a red suitcase or a pink flowered backpack such as might belong to a child.

I said how much I liked San Francisco.

He agreed. "Charming city."

"Have you been to Seattle?"

"Yes, I have," and said one of his daughters had gone to college there—not the beauty I'd met.

"Seattle feels a bit defensive..."

He was interested. "D'you think so?"

"It turns its back on the water, whereas here…"

"Yes, quite right. Fascinating," he murmured, sipping his double whiskey.

I drank my sherry and watched him unwind.

"What are you thinking?"

"You really want to know?"

"I never ask if I don't want to know," he said with a faint edge.

"I was thinking, you do all this international— work, and I'm only mildly curious. I'd like—but without urgency—to follow up on the phone call, but as for the rest, no. It surprises me. I ought to be curious, oughtn't I?"

"Perhaps I couldn't see you if you were."

Ah—new information, which seeped in over the next minutes, wiping out speech.

I drank and we ordered. So, what, I'm a plaything, like a Las Vegas showgirl you don't have to say anything to?

I guess it really does bother me that he's married. Makes me feel like a whore.

Whew. Big word.

Your choice, E. You don't have to do this.

He leaned back, smiling. "I shall ask you a question from the Game of Kings," he said.

"Polo?"

He laughed. "Succession."

Things like that tell me how American I am; I hear the first part of the word and think *success*. It wasn't just his having learned it in school. You'd have to care.

"I don't know anything about European history…" I should've realized he wouldn't embarrass me.

"You'll know this one," he said, wreathed in smiles. "Which king of England was first called 'The Bastard' and then later The Conqueror?'"

"William was the Conqueror…" *Bastard.* "Are things not going well in your negotiations?"

"Astute," he nodded, pronouncing it *a'styoot.*

"Do you want to talk?"

"Not just yet. You're so good at this I shall ask you a further question."

"And if I get it right, I get the keys to the kingdom?"

"If you'd like to have them, the shape it's in," he said. "Now, attend. Name two of the sons of William the Bastard, later William the Conqueror."

"William and Henry." I couldn't stop laughing. It must've been the sherry.

"Exactly. Very good. How did you know that?"

"Liam! It's a piece of cake."

"As a reward I shall take you to dinner. On another occasion," he twinkled.

"No keys, eh?"

"You'd have to spend millions on renovations and moving house. You wouldn't care for it."

"All right, then. I accept dinner."

"I can't stay," he said, looking at his watch, "I've a meeting at ten."

P.M. These people are so self-important: meetings at 6:00 a.m. and 10:00 p.m. Surely, the business could get done between nine and six. But this is not the sort of thing one says to a statesman. "I told you. I'm fine."

"I'd like to do a bit of touring, down to Big Sur..."

"That'd be lovely, if you have the time. Don't fret, Liam, I have a rich inner life..."

He laughed and laughed, and his unrestrained pleasure was arousing.

"However," I added, brazen, "If you'd like to come back here..."

"After midnight?" He lowered his voice.

"Why not? I don't have to work tomorrow. Though you do."

"That's a fine idea. Does it matter the time at all?"

"No. I'll read..."—what got into me?—"Gibbons' *Decline and Fall*..."

He looked quizzical, amused, and delighted in turn, impressions moving across his expressive face like weather. "I'll learn about the Kings of England," I said, "Or read Shakespeare. The tragedies. Don't worry about keeping me up."

He radiated enjoyment. His public self had to be less easy to read. It was clear that I was more intrigued by his relation to power—and his own considerable personal and sexual power—than I would like to admit. I do know this about myself, but I keep forgetting it.

The man never sleeps. He came to me at 1:20 a.m. and got up just after six, brisk, energetic. He loves his life. "I've a breakfast meeting at half eight."

"Well that's good," I said, "'Cause it's against my religion to get up before seven."

"What?" he teased, "You don't want to see the sun rise?"

"It rises," I told him, "On the other side of the country."

"What're you doing today?"

"Probably going to some museums. Or the Park."

"Have fun, then," he said. "I might not be free this evening; I'll telephone." He kissed me goodbye, and I slept another three hours.

It occurred to me that I was an ideal mistress. Nice word, eh? If he met me for dinner, fine, but if not, I wouldn't ask, wouldn't require.

I took myself to the San Francisco Museum of Modern Art. A not-beautiful day. Fog, naturally, though it'd be nice later. One of the radio stations here calls itself KFOG. I'd been wanting to see the building, had read a lot about it in the New York press. Before the Gehry opened in Bilbao, this was the first major new museum in a long time. I'd seen pictures of it, with a great funnel opening up to the sky. I had no idea where it was, took a taxi.

Extraordinary space. In which I felt tense, or perhaps expectant. Stripes of various textures, shiny and matt on the floors and walls, played havoc with my astigmatism, though thank God the galleries were white.

Nice odd windows here and there, and at the top a wonderful little catwalk made of metal mesh crossing the deep atrium. It was like looking into a broad, well-lighted well. More patterns from struts supporting the massive skylight fell onto the little bridge across the open space like insubstantial girders.

I was so happy to be here.

The sky had cleared to sharp bright blue. It was like being aloft and afloat both, like sailing on the bridge of a ship to be up there on that little glittery-white passageway, narrow as a plank out into space, the sun whitening everything. There weren't a lot of people, so I walked back and forth several times. Which is why I saw her.

Angela. With a man. Folded together like teenagers in one of the small niches I could see from the white edge of the little metal bridge.

Oh my dear God, Rory...

Her lovely hair moving like grass in a light wind.

Reflexively, I turned my back. I had to disappear, melt into a wall. I felt myself sizzling like a column of red light, pulsing and whirling, aflame, like some animate spinning thing, a little red whirlwind, calling attention to itself.

Jesus.

She would call out my name.

Of course she wouldn't.

I'm nearsighted.

I must be wrong. Had to be.

They moved out into the public space. I watched her walk. I know it. She moves with a certain sexual allure, like my Flora, a way of being both there and not, that my daughters—and I—do not have.

Like a snake.

I thought that.

Burning filled my throat. I had to get away before she saw me.

They have no money: how could she have made this trip?

It must've been really important to her…

Oh my Rory dear.

I lost my balance coming out of the museum, told myself it was the disorienting effect of the stripes on walls and floor, the barred shadows everywhere.

It was Angela.

I walked and walked after this non-encounter, shaken, no idea where I was, a mass in my throat of— what was it, anger? Yes, fury and confusion and despair.

Then it came to me and stopped my throat: I was a second choice, too.

I'd thought my marriage to Terry fell of its own weight, the weight of the children. But maybe it was this. In some sense, I was not his *wife*. His *wife* was Phoebe, the girl he'd chosen in the heat and purity and mindless summoning of youth.

My legs nearly gave way. There was no place to sit. I kept walking, drawing deep breaths and searching for the wonderful horizon: hills and buildings. I would go to the water.

I hailed a cab, said "That pier—where you can see Alcatraz?"

"Oh, sure," he said, and took me there, a tourist place with stacks of shops on brick terraces above the Bay. The place always reminds me of a painting by somebody French, and I can never remember the name of it.

Terraces with many small staircases. I went to the topmost one and got a cup of coffee in the restaurant. I took it outside and sat in the cold wind off the Bay, staring at all that blue, white sails on it, and the Bridge, Alcatraz lying offshore, none of its history showing. Like none of mine.

Garden at Sainte-Adresse.

I was glad to remember the name of it, the Monet. I felt a bit easier now, and I needed the wind, which was cold. Cleansing.

Planes of light hung between me and the water, clear, insubstantial glitter over the whole molten, glassy Bay, the mountains and the prison-island.

Sirens not too far away rose and fell, rose again, echoes of distant peaks.

Somewhere, I'd read you could hear the sound of the Sun on the Web. I'd asked Rory to find it for me, and there it was on the computer-screen. We heard it, diminished thousandsfold. Even made small enough for human hearing, it was terrible. A vast and awful roaring.

What will I do with this?

What choice've you got? Eventually the deep or ugly wound heals over, and the memory, like a stain on a white tablecloth, seeps out to the edge of the fabric, dyeing the whole thing one shade ever-so-slightly darker, the change so subtle you don't realize the color's different for years, for decades. Head and chest thudding. For maybe the first time in my life I felt empty, like the shell of an animal that has gone.

Blue. Look at the blue. Gaynell taught me that: when you're sick with grief or worry, find something beautiful, and look real hard at it.

Sometimes it's not possible.

She said it when Flora, then sixteen, said "My mother had no mother either," and I nearly fell. Her mother had had my mother, as she had me. We weren't enough. We weren't their real mothers.

As I wasn't the real wife.

It occurs to me that the Virgin was a very Jewish mother.

What does this *mean?* Of course, she was Jewish. And she would've done what? The Virgin: *that* ought to recast *Jewish mother.*

New York's been hard on me. It's a hard place for a girl from a small town in the rural

South—what *was* the rural South. Positively dizzy, I tripped getting up from the table at the pier, and nearly fell down a short flight of stairs. Shaken, I grabbed the metal railing—someone watching would've thought I was drunk—and got a cab back to my hotel.

Hole up, Charles used to say, that's what you do. You hide away in your little burrow.

Tough luck, E. Your little burrow's twenty-seven hundred miles from here.

The Institute where I trained is associated with Columbia, and once I did a workshop with college girls at Barnard, part of a longitudinal study of adaptation and change in women's life-cycles. It wasn't well-enough designed, which is too bad, because it was a really fine idea. It should've been intensive, much larger, and permanently funded.

I saw a group of eight young women four times, once each of their four years in college—should've been three times a year—and I liked doing it because even still I'm aware of my strangeness to myself during the time I spent in college before I married Terry.

I loved seeing how the young women opened out into so many changes. It was like watching a nature film, buds becoming flowers in the time it takes to draw breath.

And the point is, they changed absolutely in that time. Of course they weren't aware; it's an organic process: we change.

I wish I'd thought of this: if I'd taken photos during year one, we could've looked at them together in year four. I could have built our last meeting around them.

The changes were startling: the girls became more themselves and at the same time, on analogy with what we know from the genetics of peas and flowers, their phenotypes flourished. They would've been offended had I said it, but that's what happened. Their faces became more defined, thinner perhaps, bone-structure more visible. They were more at home in their bodies, that was part of it. They'd gotten used to them, their bodies. Taken possession of them.

This is the part I couldn't publish: the Jewish girls looked more Jewish, the Asians more Asian, and the one Latina—Marisol—ah, how her dark beauty ripened! She'd become like a visitation from one of Rivera's murals. She was at once more angular and linear, and at the same time stockier and darker in some way I cannot possibly express—her beauty was ancient and contemporary and positively breathtaking.

And what does all this have to do with Angela? I'm thinking of her early brief marriage, her—I have to assume—sexual maturity and confidence. The fact that she has become more of who she was then.

The girl I didn't know, the woman I don't know now.

I'm going to have to talk to Rory.

How *can* I? How can I possibly even *think this?*

I wanted to wail.

I was the grownup, and I'd have to decide; nobody could help me with this, though I'd no doubt get another slant when I talked with Gaynell. An image of William moved through like a benediction, momentary comfort.

I got back to the hotel so sick I lay down without taking off my clothes or makeup and fell asleep. At six the phone rang, Hauled myself into wakefulness: Liam.

"Were you asleep?"

"I think so."

"Did you have a nice day?"

"I don't know…"

"I have a dinner meeting. I can be there at nine. Is that all right?"

"Fine."

"Shall I have dessert with you?"

"Okay."

By the time he came, I was showered, composed. I'd even remembered where the spinning red figure had come from: a marvelous painting by Leonor Fini called

Red Vision, in which a floating figure made of flame hovers near and above a little-girl ghost, a white figure in a dark empty room with doorways and windows— I can't be sure of the arrangement, but I know the figure is above. As I was, on the little catwalk across the top of the museum's open space.

I'd called Gaynell and started talking about the young women in the Barnard study.

"What's going on?"

She knows me. She could hear it in my voice. I told her about seeing Angela.

A long pause before she said: "You're with a married man," adding, "why should it be different for your son's wife?"

Jesus Lord.

"Elena? You there?"

I couldn't.

"Say something, honey."

"Yeah…"

"You all right? Say something, Babe."

"I think my heart seized up."

Finally, Gaynell said: "Control's illusory, anyway."

"It's not about control," I said slowly. "I'm talking about…" I gasped, "Betrayal."

I heard her waiting.

"Well," I finally laughed, crying and shaking, "There it is. The word I hadn't thought."

Maybe because Gaynell doesn't have children, she doesn't feel aging as I do.

There's so *much* you can't say, even to your dearest friend. Some of it's not possible and some of it's beyond language; whole worlds without words. I didn't say when I thought of Angela's beautiful young face, I felt my own softening, like dough, creasing.

We're irremediably malleable. Would I prefer something that didn't change?

Naturally not, I heard myself, professional and crisp. Of course not.

When you think you can't go on, it's temporary. I know that now, fifty-plus years in. You get up. Maybe it takes two days or a week, but you get up and keep going. I know this. What I haven't figured out is the long-term cost. I'm blessed with energy. It never takes me two days. Max, eight hours.

Or: all salvation is ephemeral.

If Ciro died, it'd be longer. If a child—my hair stands up and my mouth twitches. If one of my children…I would not recover.

Liam breezed in at eleven-forty. "I find I'm able to get away. Let's drive down to Big Sur."

"Tonight?"

"Why not?"

"Because the roads are terrifying in daylight, and you're not used to driving on the right."

"You're unwilling to put your life in my hands?"

I already had. I stood, a complete blank. Finally I said, "I'd rather not, tonight. Can we go tomorrow?"

"Certainly." He nodded, and came to embrace me. "Something wrong?"

It was rather a lot to say. And anyway, I couldn't speak.

"You're a bit stiff."

"Something very…large happened today, Liam. I'd like to talk to you about it."

"All right," he said, rubbing his hands together, fresh as morning. Everything in his bearing said, Let's go; let's get on with it.

He saw himself as a problem-solver, whereas my job is to find and name. You lift the particular out of its surrounds into awareness and sometimes you get answers from the close looking.

Sometimes not.

Sometimes nothing helps.

In my line of work it's necessary not to forget this.

Well, I thought, Let's see what you can do with this one.

We went out into the cold windy night and got a cab.

In the restaurant, I told him.

"That's rough," he said.

"Yes."

He waited what seemed a long time before he said, "And what else?"

"I'm doing it." My throat wanted to close. "You're someone's Rory."

"Quite so."

I remembered having said it wouldn't mean anything to him.

It was beyond my capacity to know what it meant—what it means—to either of us.

In fact I do know. Some of it.

A marriage as old as his is central, absolutely. So this…*thing,* affair, fling, dalliance, would have to have created ripples in the lake of his marriage. It could not be without effects, however subtle, in their kitchen and their bedroom.

My presence in his life might even affirm Mary's importance; I've known people to take lovers to try to make the partner less consequential. They've needed all that closeness, but at some point it gets claustrophobic—this is usually not conscious—so they bring in someone else to open things out, to draw off some of the energy and disperse it. Electrical metaphors. Charles disparaged them. Also, what he called hydraulic metaphors, anything with water-levels. I find myself grinning: dear Charles.

The whole process is fascinating, always different, from moment to moment as well as from individual to individual. And couples, and their family histories? Geometric complexities.

And what Ciro was doing all those years—who knows?

As for Liam, who sat opposite, his face creased with attention, I thought, He may be using me in some way we both have no way of knowing.

"I keep thinking I have to tell him," I said, "Though how could I possibly? It'd be a disaster."

"Oh aye. Quite. Perhaps you could talk to her a bit?"

"That hadn't occurred to me."

"Because?"

I thought. "It'd require intimacy," I said finally, "And I don't know if I want that, with her. It might give the impression I'm willing to collude with her in..." My eyes filled. "...*Destroying* my son." I wiped them. "Wrong word."

"Probably it is the right one," Liam said.

"Well, then."

"It's always best to do less."

I nodded. Of course.

"You're not responsible," he said.

"That's right. Except with one's children...well, you have been, for such a long time, you know."

"But he's an adult."

"Yes, and he chose this woman. He knows her. He may even know this, on some level. He may need it." I winced.

"Aye."

Which, I thought later, was all he was going to say about himself and Mary. I wanted her off stage. In the dark. All senses.

"Responsibility figures heavily in negotiations," he said. "One learns to use it," and told me a good deal about his government's—his own—talks with representatives of ETA, the Israelis. I wondered about the Québécois but didn't ask.

Why was he telling me this now? Had I proved myself safe, and if so, how?

We ordered drinks and a light supper.

What difference did any of it make?

I would drink with him and sleep with him tonight, and tomorrow we would drive south, and, sun-glare off the Pacific in his eyes, maybe slide off the Coast Highway into the sea.

"Liam!" It was eight in the morning. He was at the little table in the room drinking orange juice when I came tearing out of the bathroom, "Liam!"

It takes more than an irrational woman—he looked up.

"They were threatening *you*," I said. "What an absolute dolt. I just this minute realized it."

"They," he said, patient.

"When they called—We know you know Liam"—a chill moved through me. "They were telling you our *liaison, alliance?*"—the words came in French—"was not *ours*. They were using me to…tell you they had…evidence for something and would use it." With the newspapers? With your wife? I had stopped talking. Fortunately.

"Oh aye," he said, and bent again to his newspaper.

I stood there—months after the event—toothbrush in hand, trembling.

Liam's Country

Home from San Francisco. For the first time, I thought: Terry could die. Because of seeing Angela? How odd: it's never crossed my mind. And why should it? He's not yet sixty. He runs and plays tennis and softball with a team, the children've told me.

Someday, I will die. And my children's father will die, and when we are gone, my children will have no one to comfort them. Rory and Bonita will be truly orphaned.

A current of pure need swept through me. I called her, Bonita.

When they're little, you pick them up and kiss them. You sing, you distract them. When they're older, you knock, go into their rooms and sit on their beds, and they talk to you about what's going on in their deepest hearts. And when they're grown, you make an appointment for lunch. All this time, you didn't know how much you *need* them. . .

Bonita was in the lab, of course. She has her calls forwarded, so I never know where she is: "What're you wearing?"

"What?" Ripples of laughter. Her laughter's like a clear stream, glittery and sweet and absolutely beautiful.

"It might tell me what you're doing."

"It might not. In fact, I'm wearing a black silk dress with little thin straps, but I'm in the lab checking one more measurement, then I'm going with Todd to a party." She sailed off again into laughter.

"Sexy black dress in the lab: love it!"

"That's 'cause you like incongruity."

"Good, Bon! Have a good time, honey. I hope the work's going well."

"Oh, it is. It's great. Anything special?"

"No," I lied. For most of my life, I'd been entirely comfortable lying about my own needs. It's part of that Southern acculturation: don't mind me—I've spent a lot of my professional life trying to correct for it, but not with the children.

"I'll call you tomorrow or so," she said, and I could hear the vagueness in her voice and figured she was jotting something in a lab notebook.

Then I remembered a dream from a couple of days ago: Bonita pushing a baby carriage through an exhibit in an art gallery, and she's wearing—what she's wearing is a dress I saw on Rosa MacBride once when she was on TV: a long skinny black silk dress splashed with enormous red-orange flowers; and in the dream, Bonita's hair is orange, to match the flowers. How is my daughter like Rosa MacBride?

I wandered around the apartment thinking about this, and about Liam and faithlessness, his and Angela's. And my own.

The living room needed redone. It'd gotten shabby. Had got, Liam would say. Now I wanted quiet gold-foil walls—saw them in a magazine—and an off-white sofa with scarlet cushions. Scarlet and orange and hot pink. All the colors I can't wear. That'd be amazing. Maybe one lime-green and one yellow. Extravagance, that's what I wanted.

To blot out what-all was going on?

I meandered through my rooms, thinking of brilliant colors. My suitcase lay on the floor in the study, half my stuff spilling out of it, the other half balled up on its way to the cleaner's, or ready for the laundry in plastic bags. My first night home from anywhere I sit down and call all the kids. Always have. Nine o'clock. Truth was, I wasn't up for all of them right then. I'd call the others tomorrow.

Couldn't bring myself to check the messages either, though the answering machine was flashing. I resolutely turned it so I couldn't see the light. Dan was covering; everything could wait till morning. Maybe I'd redo the bedroom and bath too. Pale sea-green and sparkly white. Next trip home, I would definitely buy furniture for the little place Ciro gave me. Fruit and flower colors: that acid green—lime—and tangerine and lemon, colors like the interiors of grapefruit— pink and yellow—and deep jewely guava. Lots of bamboo and rattan and glass.

Bamboo: one night in a hotel in London, I walk into a dining room and there, in the centre (well, we're in London) of a round table, a giant black urn, maybe six feet tall, like the kind I imagine the Dead Sea

Scrolls were found in, but without a lid; and in it, nine stalks of cane. If you didn't know you'd think they were bamboo, but I know. They're thick green jointed organic poles cut off at the tops and looking as if they're hollow, but I have sucked raw sweetness from them, so I know the chewy fibers with my mouth.

Cane. Ciro—everything. I could live there, but I don't. It's out of the question.

At midnight, I caved in and listened to the messages. Rory's said "Mom! Call up to ten-thirty. News." He'd probably had some photos accepted somewhere, maybe even a show—that'd be lovely. I went to sleep.

In the morning Fate, generous and for once gentle, delivered me from the trouble I would very nearly have caused. "We're going to have a baby," he said, his voice choked.

Oh God, I thought, and then, like a river rushing over its banks, "That's marvelous!" I'm going to be a grandmother. Oh my God. And at the same time, "Your father'll be so pleased." And then a faint silvery shadow, an image as if through tracing-paper, How do you know it's your child?

Then I thought, quite lucidly: Maybe she went there to say goodbye to someone—

That felt solid, as if something had slid into place: maybe I was right.

"If it's a girl..." he hesitated.

I didn't speak into a quite long pause. I could feel his stress in the quiet.

"I'd like to name her Phoebe," he said, soft. "Would you mind, Mother?"

"Mind? I'd love it!" By then I was crying. I remembered—he couldn't have—that fiasco with Phoebe's picture when they were little. Told him. "Have you called Bonita yet?"

"Yeah, she's really into it. Wants to be godmother and all."

"Well, sure." Then, on a plume of excitement, "Your baby might look just like your sister. When're you going to tell the others?"

"Oh, next few days," he said airily.

"When's she due? Do you know if it's a girl?"

"No, but we feel like it is. November."

"That's wonderful, Son."

Boy, was I lucky.

How could I even have *considered* it?

Saved by happenchance, Flora-lora used to call it. Yes indeed, saved by the random conjunction of sperm and egg, if not stars. What *could* I have been thinking?

The proper, or indigenous, spelling of his name is Ruairi. Liam told me. I would offer him that. By way of recompense.

Amazing: there'll be another Phoebe Summerfield in the world! I imagined a little two-year old in a flowered dress, chubby legs churning as she runs, child with a face like Rory's when little, a child named

Phoebe. What a remarkable occurrence, and of course the most natural in the world, Phoebe's germ cells down through time through her son and his wife into an unimaginable future.

Maybe new little Phoebe would look like her grandmother, the first Phoebe, who'd died so young.

Her death remains a mystery. Belief in Heaven would help. Even Hell. But as it is, I have only the permanent Earth and my paltry imagination. All deaths are beyond comprehension, but hers more than, say, Toss's.

I imagine his death: as if I had walked into his heart's deep recesses—images of interiors of body-parts. His death was a blow to the chest—and belly. First I lost my breath and then I began to be sick. I'd opened the *Times* and there it was: **"Tomás Ando, Sculptor, 59."** You don't need the verb. *To die* is understood. Or it's contextual: you read the headline, you don't need a whole lot of coaching. **"Ando Dead at 59"** is how I remembered it for a long time, but I remembered it wrong.

Paper said name, occupation, age. As if a person can be reduced to outlines, categories. What's essential? You could argue that essentials are heart, breath, the shape of the mouth. Personality. Capacities—in this case, with his hands: his art. Printed name and occupation deny flesh: as if his flesh, so dear to me at one time: how could I have walked out of there?—as if his flesh didn't matter.

It was his flesh I responded to, flesh that took up space in the world, against which I lay my head.

Lord.

After I read the obituary I imagined him in his bed, not waking up. Then, a long time later—quite recently, in fact—a client, talking about someone she worked with who'd died suddenly said, "He was just laying on the floor," and I saw Toss, not in bed, not decorous, the sheet folded over blankets and pulled up to his square brown chin, but on the floor, sprawled, awkward, who had been in life most graceful.

I felt it again, beneath my ribs, as she went on talking, verb-forms off, as most people's are. *Lie, lay. If I would have known.* Sets my teeth on edge. I had to say "Excuse me. Tell me a bit more about how well you knew him…"

Imagine being able to know, at the moment I chose Toss, what it would be like after. What *I* would be like.

I was nearly through with my training—and my marriage, and Toss, as it turns out, though I didn't know it at the time.

Oh! As I record this—I'm writing very slowly now, trying to hold on to it—I understand something absolutely new: I was tossing (*sic* and yes) all my old lines off, as a vessel about to sail casts off. Lord. All the language is weighted with my feelings…

Well! Where did I think the language *came from,* if not feeling? Acts. Which reflect and embody the deep-going…everything—

This is what aging is. The losses and the deaths collect: Phoebe's, Toss's. It's why I suddenly imagine Terry's. There's all this space now, like when the Towers came down. When buildings have been destroyed the sky's a surprise; you'd forgotten all the colors changing over the course of a day—blue to purply-pink and gold at sunset.

As if I were a microbe occupying Toss's heart I watch as it grows gray in there, all the pink diminishing and fading, the regular pulses slowing, and as color seeps away, stillness. Movement quits, but so slowly it's undetectable at first. Then the muscle goes inert, the grayed walls dull, begin to cool, and finally it's like being inside a walk-in meat-locker, irremediably cold.

That's how Toss died.

Or maybe his heart whirled in its thin sac like a cyclone moving into the Indian Ocean off Durban, the hot steamy cloud spinning smaller and smaller until it's a crystal, brilliant as diamond, and then in a flash it devolves: diamond to coal to bit of ash. *Poof,* a speck, driven on the wind to someplace foreign, someplace nobody's there to recognize it. A stretch of dunes in Namibia, say.

That's what our lives are anyway. We're made of stardust.

It's beyond comprehension: a man who I loved, who I had taken into my body, who occupied my heart and most sacred spaces, is dead under the earth. It takes great concentration to really believe it, and sometimes I'm not capable of it.

Sometimes I can imagine what comes after. Phoebe Two will live into the last part of the century—maybe 2093 or some unimaginable number which will be the daily address of people who live then, our descendants. But oh my God, anything could happen to her—anything.

I see people crushed in train wrecks, mothers keening over dead children. Starvation, terror, dismemberment.

Ciro's daughter. The men with the cameras. It's not that much of a leap, is it.

Hostages to fortune. Gaynell said that's why she and Coleman never had children, quoting Francis Bacon. The man knew something, she said, but I'm sure Gaynell and Coleman have other reasons as well.

Liam's familiar warmth on the phone. He almost never called: once after the threat, once to arrange our liaison in San Francisco, perhaps two other times. Now he said, "I just read one of your stories, Elena."

"What? Liam!" I laughed. "I have information to adjust to, here."

"In a magazine my daughter gave me."

Everything went still.

"'Halcyon,' Elena Summerfield. You never said."

"On a plane?" I asked, bizarrely—even I realized this. But when did he have time to read, except on planes?

He laughed. That full-throated free laughter.

"Well," I said.

"Accomplished." I heard the smile in his voice, saw him nodding.

"Thank you."

"Have you written about us?"

"Li-am. I *make   it   up.*"

"Indeed?"

"One has to." Now I laughed. Relief, probably.

What a strange conversation, I thought, imagining an arrow—not Cupid's—going straight out into space, like radio waves, direct to the zenith. Where was he?

Wherever that is—we're rotating so the zenith must keep changing. Depends on where you are, I told myself. I think I was trying to ground myself—by thinking of space? Lord. Then I thought, Maybe the universe is circular—it's not. It's an ellipse, far as we know—an elongated pancake. I laughed, pulling myself back: "Where are you?"

"Oh," as if it were a startling question. "On an airplane. Calling from—em—let's see. I suppose somewhere over Greenland. Yes." His voice thinned. "I can see an iceberg down there."

"Amazing!" Liam. My heart filled.

"Sea's quite green today."

"Which direction?"

"The sea?"

Now I couldn't control my laughter. "Are you flying in."

"East."

Afterward I thought, You really do have a weird mind, E. It did not occur to me to say Where are you going?

"Send me some others, will you?"

"Shall I?"

"Yes." There was the peremptory: if I say it I mean it.

"But…"

"I shall enjoy them. I'd like to have them."

"All right, Liam. Be well."

My head filled with images of mines and tripwires—from TV news. Doubtless he read political philosophy and history, but I didn't know what else he read. I knew nothing about him.

How could it be nothing when I know the texture of his flesh, his scent—his body?

It would be childish—even absurd—for him to want them as totems, bits of my mind and spirit, but that's what I thought, showering and getting into my bed made up with fresh sweet-smelling linens that night.

I was in Paris once for nine days and can't remember any of it.

No, I remember the river and the museums and some narrow leafy streets near the Sorbonne, and my hotel room, but I can't remember a single restaurant, a single meal. There were people from the conference; I remember some of them. I remember being at Le Deux Magots on a cool, sunny day. I sat outdoors sketching the church across the street into my notebook—it was half-obscured by green—and along came a TV crew with a guy holding one of those mop-head booms, tatty guy in jeans with camera, and a skinny *directrice* in the requisite skinny black clothes. It was right after Liam, and I suppose I wasn't yet ready to turn my gaze outward.

He had called me his wild temptress. That's what filled my mind in Paris, and his having pinned me. I lay beneath him after sex. He withdrew and crouched above me on his knees, his palms pressing mine, and he looked down at me and said I was his wild temptress. I was aware at the time of the light in the room and his thighs pressing, his soft penis and the sac dangling. I wanted to hold him there with both hands, I wanted to fill my hands with him but he had me pinned, and there was a sharp brief surge of something like anger.

When he said it, I thought, madly, it had to do with my hair, registering "tress," a fashion word he'd never use, and not "tempt"—because, I think now, who'd want all that *—consequence?*

My hotel room had a massive antique armoire with three mirrors stained by age, and a tiny French balcony with tall glass and wrought-iron-trimmed doors to the ceiling. I kept them open to hear street sounds. Sounds like New York.

In Versailles to see the gardens, I think I realized my mind had been emptied by Liam's having moved through it. Like a hurricane, he wiped out all the furniture standing around.

I walked in the gardens and understood *sublime.*

My wild temptress.

I remember Lausanne at dusk. Hills of course. The lake. Which is Evian in France. I grew up too poor to pay for water, but my children buy it, celebrity water. If not for zoon-lenses, we wouldn't have this stupid pervasive rush to celebrity. I wonder what will follow it...

The Swiss hotel had a lovely restaurant, with big windows that opened onto the street. Couldn't imagine what it'd be like in winter. A man walking down the steep street stopped to speak to someone at the next table. I suppose I liked the way inner and outer met. There was wonderful butter and pretty china. I'd left the conference, and before that I'd left Liam, and before that I'd left the States and my ordinary life.

When you get on a plane to go to a conference, you don't wonder how you will be changed by whatever's going to happen. I feel, the older I get, a part of myself reaching out into the future, for what it has for me. Stupid, because in a few years—too few—it'll be delivered to me like a battered package, the terminus, and I will understand it in a way I can't now, though I think about it a lot, unfortunately.

Ciro once said You have to be optimistic. After what-all he's been through?

Why? I did not say back.

One of my clients is a college-age woman from Colombia who lives on Park Avenue in one of her family's many homes. She talks about her huge family, seven aunts and uncles on one side and ten on the other. They all gather, and all the children—her cousins—at Christmas at the finca in the mountains of Colombia. "Doesn't the altitude bother you?" I ask, imagining dozens of rich supremely confident young people in khaki shorts and white shirts and Birkenstocks, expensive sweaters tied around their shoulders, who've flown out of New York and L.A. and D.C., where she's said the family's concentrated, all carrying Vuitton luggage, all speaking beautiful spectacularly fast Spanish.

"No." She smiles her brilliant smile, white teeth, jet eyes twinkling. She says she's a snob about her Spanish, speaks it like a European, and I think it's a colonial thing she's learned from her rich family, and then she produces a rippling sequence in the most elegant Spanish I have ever in my life heard. Something in the way her lips curve around the sounds brings Ciro into my consulting room.

"I have a friend from Cuba."

"Cubans don't pronounce their consonants as we do. You know: not only dialect, but the vocabulary's different from European Spanish."

I nod. Spanish speakers in this hemisphere have their own national dialects, she says. I know it, but as I search my memory I can't hear any difference, and one day getting out of a cab in Midtown, when a man started to get in as I was gathering my things, I exclaimed "¡Momento, por favor!" surprising myself.

A Tuesday in October. Bright and crisp, a little too cool for me, foretaste of winter. My first client's at ten. I pick up a cinnamon roll and come in at 8:40 and turn on WQXR but there's too much talk, so I put in a CD. Beethoven sonatas keep me company while I make coffee and settle down with the paper, which I bought on Fifty-eighth Street and have carried east and north to my office. I check my calendar. Hair appointment at four. I'd forgotten it. I open the paper and flip through the pages. The article's on 3, International News.

Even if it were on the front page I might not have seen it because I tend not to scan. I miss a lot of news that way, and anyway, I carried it folded up.

It occurs to me that I have always expected it.

European Union Minister Killed

I can't breathe. I have risen from my chair. I'm holding the edge of my desk, heart knocking, running downhill over sharp rocks, pulling me with it. I'd read it before I was aware, and I know.

BRUSSELS, October 8 (Reuters)—Liam Stephenson, Minister to the European Union, was shot dead early Saturday by an unknown assailant. Mr. Stephenson, 58, was attending meetings of the European Union. [Further details are unavailable.]

For days I walk around with a weight on my chest, sudden sweats, sudden tears, my skin grainy and terrible, as if I hadn't slept for weeks.

I feel ill in ways I can't locate, as if I've a low-grade fever, which perhaps I have.

Liam dead by gunshot.

Early on Saturday.

On his way to a woman?

It's entirely possible, but it's irrelevant, doesn't mitigate my grief or tilt it into anger.

Murdered.

Shot dead on the street like an animal.

What was I doing? It was late Friday night here. I was sleeping. All these hours—all these days—I was walking through my life, and he was dead.

He was dead. And I didn't know it.

How could that be? The recalcitrant child I had long ago abandoned was stamping her foot and shouting, How?

Happens all the time.

Days later when I talk to Michael he will say, "Animals don't walk the streets, Momma," and we laugh until I end in tears.

Sometimes it's a kind of hollowness, like numbness, sometimes it rages through me with enormous power, obliterating everything.

The grief is immediate—*unmediated*: pours like tides: swells and shallows, crests and troughs and sprays, the sudden weeping.

Stinging in my nose, head stuffed up, as if I had a cold. And underlying all of it, a subtle malaise that feels like something's profoundly wrong with me. "There is," Gaynell says. "You're in pain. You're sick with grief. You need to treat yourself cleverly."

"It wasn't even about *him*," I say.

She waits.

"It was at the EU. It wasn't even about events in his home country."

"You don't know that."

"That's right." I don't know anything.

One night I woke to find myself upright in bed: now he'll never think of me. All the aspects of me when I was with him, laughing, aroused, tense, thoughtful— all the facets that Liam evoked. Parts of me, then. Died with him; his memories of me were physical. Synapses are. His death erased little organic electric particles of me.

My wild temptress. The most extraordinary thing anybody's ever said to me.

Everything he knew—about his country and its politics, about his wife and their children. In his head, the unique arrangements of his experience, songs, dumb jingles, political threats, advertisements—like the one we saw in San Francisco: *Why does El Niño keep coming back?* A few miles later: *For the cheese—* all that has been obliterated.

Someday it'll be Ciro, and I won't be able to stand it.

I need for him to be here, walking around, talking. On his damned cellphone.

Ciro.

Ah, Liam, where *are* you?

Each day, brilliant and inventive, my subconscious finds yet another way to think about him.

How can he be nowhere?

His name emerges without volition from my mouth. On several days I shock myself, calling his name aloud. Liam.

How could you leave without telling me?

I talk to him.

I didn't need you in my arms, I needed you in the world.

Why do we speak directly to the dead?

It's a denial of their implacable silence?

Li-am. Asleep under the earth.

Finally a day will come when I can say to myself as much as to him: Rest in peace, Liam, but this is months away, unimaginable.

The papers say he died at the hands of a young French-born German named Michel Kauffmann who went to high school in L.A., returned to Europe, and was presumed to have ties to a neo-Nazi organization.

Goes on all the time. I live in New York: terror, drugs, random murders *every single day*. Children killed when bullets ricochet off brick apartment buildings. Madmen push people off subway platforms. Children suffocate while their mothers are out looking to score. Guns.

Don't get me started.

Mind is fascinating. Which is why I study it. As if I am an outline, a receptacle for human *stuff,* whatever's evoked—mothering, sexuality, needs for mastery, autonomy, professionalism—all this, as needed—fills in the outline and walks out into the world or into the arms of the beloved, and makes new experience. She leaves behind all the other people who compose me standing around like Segal sculptures, living and inanimate both.

That's right: waiting to be animated by need, presence, volition, mine or others'. Things you don't need to *learn,* things you just know to do, to be. They occupy you and fill you.

So now I am a woman grieving.

One day apropos of nothing I could name, not a scent, not an image, I remembered Toss and other English speakers I've known from the Southern Hemisphere. From the last of Empire: they don't say "gotten." Toss had been here seven years by the time I knew him and he still said "got" where we'd say "gotten." After Liam died I realized they shared this. And they were both of them dead.

Sometime after this I dreamed a gavotte, formal and regular. Its formality was clearly a metaphor for intercourse, a schematic. And although dance stands in for the coming together, I'd never thought of it that way, consciously.

Gaynell had said "You'll have to tell them, the kids."

"I know." I began to laugh. "What? Tell them a married man I was sleeping with has been murdered and it's really bent me outta shape?"

"He mattered," she said.

During our regular conversations I managed to ask each of them, "Did you read that thing in the paper about the E.U. minister shot in Belgium?"

Bonita had. "Why?"

"I knew him," I said, thinking about the Biblical *to know.*

"Oh, that's awful," Bonita said. "How'd you happen to?"

"Remember when I was in Europe and gave that talk? He showed me around. Met him then."

"Oh, so it was casual?" Keen child, Bonita. She's always had an uncanny connection to what I'm feeling.

Each of them reads me well. Differently, but well.

I'd have to lie.

Couldn't say No, I loved him.

Even to myself I have to say *love affair*. And now that he was gone I was certain that's what it was.

"I knew him pretty well," I said.

"Oh, Momma," she said, "Sorry," and I saw her face and soft light hair—at a window.

"Are you at a window?"

"No." She sounded startled. "Why?"

"I miss you. I'm imagining you at a window, darling."

I remembered Liam's fussing one night, about having to work—I'd thought it was politeness. Now I could let myself know: he wanted to be with me.

Why does someone's death bring waves of new understanding?

"It's so strange," I told my colleague Dan over lunch. "You can always imagine yourself fantasizing someone, but not someone else fantasizing you."

I worried this for days: being the subject—and object—of another's dream-wishes, his fantasies.

Caroline and Sarah, Rory and Michael and Flora didn't know, so I had to tell each of them. "A man I know—a friend—died. By gunshot." Or "...was shot to death." They responded warmly, each from her or his own temperament. Caroline said, "Oh again," her voice baffled by dismay. For her it's as if I knew Phoebe. Sarah too: "Not again, Ma."

By the time I tell Michael I'm able to joke, "I'm going to have to quit paying my NRA dues."

"You don't think everybody ought to have guns?" he says, mock-incredulous, and that's when he says animals don't prowl the streets, but he's wrong.

I never forget Toss's death—it's been a presence since I learned it, as now Liam's will be. At some point you're too old to forget things. If your mind hasn't quit.

This is different from "I'll always remember my first love, what's-his-name?" His name seems to be Ciro, and if he were to be gone from the world I would be bereft utterly.

Bonita calls one night to say she's moving. "Guess where, Momma?"

"Montreal?" I think Simi Valley and shrink a bit. Don't go far, Dumpling.

"South."

She's already in Raleigh. "Atlanta?"

"South of Montreal, north of Atlanta." She laughs.

"New York's too much to hope for."

"Boston!"

"Boston! Oh great, sweetheart!"

"Angela said I could help with the baby." Then, soft, "I hope I'll have my own babies one day…"

I do too.

"There'll be a lot of interesting men in the Boston area," I tell her, thinking It's time. Everybody's in motion. Flora will move to Chicago and Michael will finish school and leave there.

Bonita will be near her brother in Boston. A gathering: Rory and Bonita together, as on some level they always are, and Angela. If they name the new baby Phoebe, they'll all be together again, Rory and Bonita and Phoebe, but inverted, Rory and Bonita the grownups.

I think about telling Gaynell and how appreciative she'll be. Her eyes will widen and she'll say, "That is *remaaarkable*," in her low familiar drawl. But when I think about telling Dan I don't want to. He'll say something abstract and reductive and useless like They're reconstituting the original family.

And if they do reconstitute the original family, what?

And if Angela loved someone before she loved Rory, does it matter?

Early November, an event. The phone rang in my office. "Dr. Elena Summerfield."

"I am Mary Stephenson."

Wires twanged in my head. It took fully two or three seconds to realize who she was.

"How are you?" I said, a reflex. Immediately I was caught up in imagining: their voices at night, that intimacy, the burr of his baritone, her light descant. Her hand, unselfconscious, on his thigh. The ease of the long-together. Sounds my children might've been mystified by, when I lived with Terry. Talk. Because it's natural we don't credit its power to keep us together.

"I'm calling because I found your name in my husband's address book…"

Oh my Lord.

"I thought you should know. My husband was shot to death…"

"Oh, Mrs. Stephenson, I know. I read it. I'm so sorry!"

Dumbest words in the history…all we have.

I couldn't breathe.

"We're fine here," she said, deliberate.

"Your husband was a vibrant man. He…" What? Will be terribly missed? Contributed to world peace?

My mind, completely empty, filled with formula, phrases without specificity; useless, insulting.

It wasn't possible to offer comfort.

"He did quite important work and his life was wasted," she said.

What have I learned from the gift of time I've given myself—from writing this? A ton of things I couldn't put into words—except that I have.

It's a collection of snapshots, a photo-album of one life. Ciro giving me the beach— I'd never thought, of Ciro's having given me the beach, that he was capable of great dramatic gestures. That I am.

I hadn't known—

How could I have?

From miles up we're little ants scurrying: you couldn't even imagine individuals. But our consciousness has been designed for each of us, so that's what we attend to.

My one life, ordinary as bread, has been drenched with beautiful surprises, extraordinary events, generous gifts. How could this fail to dazzle?

My children.

And Liam. Liam, who could call and say, Will you by any chance be in San Francisco? as if it didn't nearly drive the ship of his marriage onto shoals studded with granite.

Eight months later there was a two-inch piece at the bottom of a page filled with war-zone photographs: **No Ties to Nazi Group.** *(BERLIN, June 10 Agence Presse)—Michel Kauffmann, the radical killer of Liam Stephenson, Minister to the European Union, was found not guilty of membership in the New Socialist*

Order, a neo-Nazi group suspected by the German government of having violated national anti-discrimination laws. A promising polymath, Kauffmann knew Chinese and Vietnamese as well as French, German, and English. He is serving a twenty-five-year sentence for the murder. Sources say he will likely be released after serving five to seven years.

That piece—and Michel Kauffmann in jail, opened something in me. It didn't happen right away, and it didn't give me peace—of course not. I kept thinking of palm trees. Liam was gone, and in the volume of his absence I stood with him again in the wind on the coast, freezing and happy, seeing less and less as my glasses got salted by spray blowing in off the sea. There was an intensity between us it has taken me all this time to recognize. We leaned into one another—over meals, having a cup of coffee, walking. If I'd been someone watching us, that's what I would have seen.

I was in it, and did not see.

But I felt it, the intensity that wrapped us like a dense nonmaterial fabric shot through with glitter and made—not of something rare and expensive—no. Something made from the daily and ordinary, a man and a woman. Cotton, perhaps, or wool. Better: wool, which has no associations with slavery—that I know of.

Periodically the issue of restitution—usually with respect to Nazi war crimes—comes up. Someday soon all the remaining principals will be dead, and the questions will be different. A Jew, I have often asked myself what I think, and interrupted my training one day to argue quite heatedly with Charles about it. He thought it was symbolic and necessary. I thought it was an empty gesture. Worse, an ugly one, because it asserts that money can balance life.

In my head where everything's as viscous as Cuban black bean soup, and just about as dark and lumpy, restitution mixes with punishment and forgiveness. Ham and onions, black beans. Liam is dead and this man Kauffmann lives. Do I wish him dead as well? No. But this man can look up to blue skies, clouds moving across them. The sun gets in his eyes. He's in the world. He's somewhere.

Sometimes—in my image of nets flung over the world—the sparkles at the junctures are ensigns of Liam's country. Sometimes they mark all the places we'd been together, bright, shining, red silk, shattering blue, viridian, gold They send their little ripples out, splashes of color marking the daily: they snap in the wind, images of energy sending up happy noises.

Over time the sound diminishes, but while I live I'll hear them.

THE MEN IN MY LIFE

Aloft

I'm back in Sarasota because my stepmother has died. Softly. Lucky woman slipped out of a chair at a bingo game after dinner with friends. This is why I can't get old: I don't play bingo and hook rugs and watch television. I don't think there are nursing homes where the Muzak plays Purcell or Buxtehude and the game room shelves are full of books.

I'll have things to do at the bank and her apartment. Ciro is out of town when I call from the airport to tell him, but I leave word and sure enough, half an hour doesn't pass before he telephones. I'm standing at the car-rental counter.

"I'll come back. I'll walk you through things at the bank. I know everybody there."

"Where are you?"

With satellite-phones you can get calls from anywhere. You can get e-mail from Sierra Leone in less than two-point-five minutes and not know where it came from. When Ciro gets his messages, he might be in Xian.

"New South Wales."

"Seriously?!"

He laughs. "Just south of Lakeland."

"All right, come back then. I'll make reservations and leave word."

"I'll pick you up."

"I think I need a car, Ciro."

"See you tomorrow, then."

It's amazing how he avoids conflict. Something learned recently? Soc departments ought to offer courses in it—they do in Liam's country. It'd stand youngsters in good stead—might cut down on the physical violence in young men, and couldn't hurt in marriages, either.

We learn so late.

I get in the rented car, and then, as if I had the entire plan for the condo in my head, on the way south from the airport I stop at a furniture store on the North Trail, where I buy two small grass-green sofas, a glass dining-table with a rattan base and six matching chairs, a queen-sized bed, a bistro table for the kitchen, and two chairs, and two small white chests of drawers.

My mental list adds things like mattress pads, sheets, towels, dishes, flatware, but I'm finished for now. I'll get them on St. Armand's Key one of these days. It feels good to sign the credit-slip, as if I've accomplished an unwelcome task. I get back in the car and head for the beach.

I do not own a suit. Once did, but they're not congenial to my spirit. So I stride into the bank in a soft gray dress with a full swirly skirt, lizard spike-heels and chunky gold and amber beads, closest thing I have to power-clothes. Ciro is waiting in the Trust

Department lobby, a gleaming overdone place designed to reassure people their money's being well looked-after, as mine has been. Now that Anna-Louise is dead I am the recipient of what's left. My sisters took under my mother's and father's wills when they died, but there were funds set aside for me—because of all those children?—an equal-if-bizarre arrangement I'd like to imagine was dreamed up by my dark knight, who kissed me lightly and accompanied me into the meeting with the bank people.

 Finally we were finished. Drained. I felt like an empty swimming pool, painted cement surface dried and cracking in the sun.

"You're a rich woman, Elena," Ciro said, his hand on my back as we left the conference room and its massive mahogany table.

How could I take pleasure in it? "They made it from nothing."

"They worked hard," he nodded.

It stung, my parents' hard lives and my easy one. And now a softer old age than I could've managed by myself.

"All that business makes me real tired, all that phony handshaking and so-nice-to-*see*-you."

"Didn't show," he said.

"Did it not?"

"You're very...competent," he said.

I stared. Competent's what you say when someone's a barely adequate therapist. A crummy writer. He must've seen something on my face, adding, "It was a compliment, Sweetheart," and opened the door.

"Thank you," I said, trying.

I hadn't quite left the meeting. It was what my life would've been, had I stayed here: Miz Summerfield, how *nice* to see you…

It's not phony, and it works well, but it's not me.

Styles. Surfaces. No wonder I keep coming up against them. We walked out into the winter sunshine.

I squinted and looked up. He stood beside me on the pavement. Sometimes men are enormously patient, I think. I gathered my energies. "So now I have to think you're with me for my money," I said.

"You can depend on it," he said with a formal little bow.

I laughed and kissed him, right there on the street. He didn't like it. "Sorry."

Then he laughed and I could see arousal in his eyes, "No, you're not," he said, holding me around the shoulders, hard.

"I love your mouth."

"Mouth," he echoed, ironic.

"As in boca *grrrande,*" I rolled the *r* wonderfully. That was probably wrong. Not the word for the human mouth.

He laughed. "Fresh."

We went to lunch at one of his private clubs in a tall building not far from the bank. The skies were beautiful, shiny enamel with huge piles of white gold-bright hot-weather clouds. We were so high up that even from where we were, downtown, it was possible to see the Gulf.

"I just realized," I said, and I felt my eyes tearing.

He didn't speak.

"I bought furniture for the condo yesterday, on my way from the airport."

He looked a bit perturbed.

"Now I'll have my own home here," I managed.

He nodded.

The waiter came and he ordered a Scotch and salad.

"Can I have a sip of your drink?"

"I'll get you your own."

Of course he would.

What I really needed was to drink from his glass. "Just the merest sip," I said, tasting. "Actually, I should buy you lunch," I said, "Now that I'm rich."

"You can't. My club."

Had any other man ever enjoyed feeding me as much as he does?

While we ate he told me how I ought to invest the money. At the bank, I'd said I wanted them to continue to manage it all.

I listened.

He wiped his lips with the edge of the napkin, fastidious man, and leaned back. I looked out the window at the sky and the Gulf, equally blue.

"I know what let's do."

I waited.

"Fly to the other coast."

"Any special reason?"

"Everest."

"Okay."

"I'll call and arrange it," he said, taking the cellphone from his pocket.

"What do you have to do, tell them to fuel it?"

"Got to get the pilot out there."

"You don't fly it yourself?"

"Can't. Heart."

Blue parachute silk, torn and tearing. Tissue-thin, with blood-vessels and capillaries.

"We ought to fly to Cuba!"

"You have to file a flight-plan," he said.

I thought about the risk. I'd do it, fly to Cuba. He would not.

En Español he said his father would bless such an intemperate expedition. I watched his beautiful lips produce the Spanish.

My young Colombian client had said most American Spanish is blurry, its sentences held together by clear vowel-sounds. But Ciro speaks like a Conquistador. It's a class thing.

"I wish I spoke your language better," I told him. "I speak gringo Spanish..."

He looked shocked. He's a bit of a prude, is Ciro, so I wasn't surprised when, gently rebuking, he said "Means 'white man's Spanish.'"

I laughed, embarrassed. "Frijoles negros," I said, remembering, *Tu Español suena como frijoles negros.*

"What were you doing in New Guinea?" This is the way our conversations move: he says something, and years later when I ask about it he's not surprised.

"Buying furniture. I got a wonderful late-seventeenth century cabinet from Southeastern China, lattice-work, absolutely unique. Paid $62,000 for it."

Without shipping, I thought, suppressing the urge to laugh.

"Made of a beautiful wood called huanghuali."

So it wasn't stained by his daughter's death. He could keep things separate. So much about him—about everybody—is beyond me. Planes I could understand, deep-sea fishing, boats and houses. Furniture? I said, "I reckon you'd have to furnish all those houses," and glanced at the Rolex.

"And in Hawai'i," he said, "I found a wonderful Philippine screen."

I laughed. I couldn't help it. "How do you keep track of which house your things're in?"

He grinned.

I thought: He talks in numbers, odds and risk. *I have forty percent of my heart.*

And all of mine, I do not say.

Can it be all? In fact it's in flux, my own tissue-paper heart. Moves like water-clouds without my will—from this man to Liam, from Terry to Toss to where I am today. I am swept by awareness: I am indeed fortunate.

"Something wrong?"

"Oh. No."

"You got a bit pale."

"I'm fine. Ciro, I was thinking about that island—Soufrière?—in the Caribbean with the volcanic eruption..."

"Saint Lucia. We're not going that far south."

"Did you know it's possible to hear earthquake activity as a tone?"

"Ah yes, B♭," he said, amusement pulling at his mouth. Then he said, "When that volcano goes, plumes rise forty thousand feet, and you've got to clear air-traffic."

"Butterflies' wings," I nodded.

"And the roar of the Sun. People are recording it. Emilio," he said, naming a son, "Saw it on the Web, made sure I saw it."

I was astonished into silence.

"Let's go. You ready?" He wiped his mouth again. I resisted running my finger—or putting my mouth—on it.

We drove out to the airport, Ciro on the car-phone checking messages, giving buy and sell orders, talking to the pilot, guy named Francisco. He turned to me. "Has anybody told you what a fresh mouth you have?"

"You did. Besides, I haven't said anything."

"You were about to."

I blew him a kiss. "Frequently," I said.

"I didn't ask how often."

I laughed. "In New York it's called *attitude.*"

"You really care for it there?"

"My practice is there." We crossed the DeSoto Road. "Used to be, the end of town was out here." We'd lived out here for a couple of years when I was a child, in a rented house on pastureland surrounded by a fence and seven Brahman cattle. One bull. That should've taught me something.

"How important is it?"

"It's how I earn my living," I said.

Nobody knows how important it is, my work, I was thinking as we drove.

I watched scrubby palms and palmetto whizz past, back for a moment in that little house, those nights when we were young—my parents younger than I am now—the cattle at night like clouds come to earth, friendly white presences in the dark that painted out the fence. There was no way I could know how serious the question was, and when I did, I remembered having told William: *I do not know men.*

Which cost me a great deal, but also made it possible for me not to have to choose.

He turned on the news. I should've remarked that but didn't, because what we heard then moved into my mind and occupied all the space in it, as an accident erases everything that's happened just before it. A child had been found in a car twelve hours after her mother and uncle died in an accident in the woods up near Micanopy, near Gainesville. Haven't been there since I was young.

It's real different up there. No palm trees, lots of live-oak, Spanish moss draped over everything. North Florida has a much more rural feel than the coasts. I remember going there for homecoming weekends: football games in the rain—in my best dresses. Before I met Terry I went with Warner, my high school boyfriend. Everybody was drunk most of the weekend, and there were those mash-you-together dances afterward.

Lord, talk about puberty rites.

At Warner's fraternity: fried chicken and kale, scrambled eggs with ketchup, cornbread, cobbler, and ice-cream. Combinations ought to be outlawed.

The child was three or four. What would she remember of a long dark night in a car alone crying for her mother who couldn't answer?

I think of it as *the day Ciro and I flew across the state.*

At the airport he slowed to take a curve and we saw a little bug-looking thing flying, all its struts and frets showing, like an airplane version of a swamp buggy. "What's that thing looks like a praying mantis?"

"Ultra-light," he said. "Runs on a quarter-horsepower engine."

"Like a lawnmower."

"Your average lawnmower doesn't fly."

"Mine certainly doesn't. Have you ever been up in one?"

"Used to fly them," he said.

I laughed: "Ciro and the levitating lawnmower…"

"Breezies, gliders, lots of light craft…"

"It must be like real flight."

"Say what?"

"There's not a lot between you and the air."

"That's why people like it."

"I'd be terrified."

"But you'd do it," he said.

I looked into his dark eyes. "Thank you."

That's what I've been doing: not flying or skydiving but taking the few men I wanted as they've offered themselves to me, taking emotional risks, I suppose. Going where my energies converge.

"Loren has one," he said, of another son.

"You let him fly one of those things?!"

He grinned.

"I wouldn't stop my son from doing it either, but I sure would hate it."

"I don't love it," he said.

His airplane was very small, not much more solid than the breezy, silver with bright red trim. He introduced me to the pilot, a skinny mustached man with a spotty beard, then he helped me in, saw to it that I was buckled and had my earphones on so we could talk over the engine noise.

He held my hand all the way to Palm Beach.

"There's your lake," I told him looking below to ruddy grasses, structures that wouldn't've been there forty years ago. "There's your irrigation system."

"Immigrants value the land," he said.

"When I was ten," I told him, "I read an ad for land near the Everglades. Something like $50 an acre, I don't remember…my father didn't have an extra fifty dollars."

"Your father began with nothing. When he died he was a substantial man."

"Like your father." Like you.

What'll I leave? A few heart-filling moments with my children, a few sharp insights in the treatment-room? A dozen short stories.

Not a whole lot.

The grasses are golden this time of year, and red. We flew over rivers snaking and looping, creeks and streams like glimmering strings in hazy sun. "I love flying this low, you get to see all the land features," I told him, but I didn't like the heavy earphones, having to talk to him through machinery when he was right next to me.

He handed me a map and pointed. North to south a series of lakes east of the Ridge gleamed in sunlight like pewter coins. We were heading south and east toward the ocean, but not far enough south to fly over the grassy inland sea. Some time I'd love to fly low over the Everglades. Below, the hungry browned greens of winter; the groves bright spots in the russet, gold and green, Florida's permanent green, burnished red and sunwashed gold.

Some distance out, I was thinking of his sons, he'd shown me photos. They look just like him, as if they hadn't needed a mother. I was trying to remember what I'd learned a hundred years ago about daughter-cells, copies, DNA made visible, when he spoke. His voice, sudden and loud in the headphones, shook me—the wind and motor-noise had put me in a kind of trance. I jumped.

"I didn't mean to frighten you." It seemed I felt rather than heard this. I watched the beautiful mouth.

"What did you say?"

"Nothing."

I asked again.

He murmured it, a ribbon of speech through engine noise: "No me mires por la ventana." Don't look out the window at me.

He stroked my cheek, encumbered by the earphones. I remember I frowned and said again, What?

He kissed my arm, below the elbow, where it's white and blue and the skin is thin. It felt like farewell.

Don't look out the window at me.

It was a tragedy. Not the sort of tragedy that left the little girl in the wreck waiting for her momma to wake up when she never would, and not the tragedy that took Terry's wife and my children's mother before they could know her.

This was something other—

We had worked really hard for fifty years to remedy what we'd thought was our unsuitability. We had remade ourselves, and when we were finished we were no longer people who could be together.

Heartfelt thanks
to my son Peter Linett and to Erika Menanteaux
for help with the Spanish
to my daughter Maren Linett for an important
suggestion
to Chris Gordon Owen for her most helpful
conversations
to Susan Wegener for her many
contributions of great value
and to
Anne McCrary Sullivan, Ann Folwell Stanford,
Babo Kamel, K. Alma Peterson, Patricia Corbus
for their special gifts

About the Author

Deena Linett was born in Boston to first-generation American parents and grew up on the Gulf coast of Florida. After earning the doctorate at Rutgers University while raising her three children, she became a college teacher and has been publishing fiction, essays, and poetry since that time. Her work has been recognized and enhanced by fellowships to Yaddo, Hawthornden Castle, Scotland, and The Baltic Centre for Writers and Translators. The Scotland and Baltic Centre residencies have given her the material for four collections of poems, the latest in 2018, *Translucent When Fired: Poems New & Selected.* Her first three novels each won small national contests.

Also by Deena Linett

On Common Ground
The Translator's Wife
Rare Earths
Woman Crossing a Field
The Gate at Visby
Translucent When Fired
What Winter Means

About the Press

Unsolicited Press is based is Portland, Oregon. The small press got its start in 2012 and is operated by incredulous volunteers. The team produces literary nonfiction, fiction, and poetry from emerging and award-winning authors.

Learn more at www.unsolicitedpress.com.